DRUMMING UP WORLD MUSIC

WEST AFRICA

SENEGAL · GUINEA · MALI
NIGER · BURKINA FASO

A Rhythm Hunters Adventure

BY LINDSAY RUST & STEVE CAMPBELL

DANCING DRUM

NOTE: "Drumming Up World Music: West Africa" should include a **CD and DVD**. If there are no discs attached inside the cover of this book, email **info@dancingdrum. com** to request your copies at no additional charge. Please include your shipping address, and let us know where you purchased the book.

Published by:
DANCING DRUM
P.O. Box 91841
Santa Barbara, CA
93190-1941 USA
www.dancingdrum.com

Photographs and illustrations by Lindsay Rust & Steve Campbell, except where noted otherwise.

ISBN-13: 978-0-9816724-3-4
ISBN-10: 0-9816724-3-4

Library of Congress Control Number: 2010930699
Printed in the United States of America.

CONTENTS

INTRODUCTION

TRAVEL JOURNALS

SENEGAL

GUINEA

THE MUSIC

VISUAL ART PROJECTS

ADDITIONAL RESOURCES

DRUMMING UP WORLD MUSIC

WEST AFRICA

BY LINDSAY RUST & STEVE CAMPBELL
DANCING DRUM

ACKNOWLEDGEMENTS

This book would not be possible without the many excellent teachers that we have studied with over the years. Very special thanks and gratitude are due to Abdoul Doumbia, Abdoulaye Diakite, Moussa Traore, Bolokada Conde, Dramane Kone, Bara M'Boup, Vieux Traore, Sitan Traore, the members of Lilidya, Yacouba Moumouni, Adamou Daouda (Nagouli), Abdoulaye Alhassane, Harouna Abdou, Housseini Chibakou, Katherine Onadja, Fatou Amadou, Bioma Sanogo, Salif, Yacouba Siri, Abdoulaye Cantara, and the hundreds of people who have taken the time to share their music and culture with us.

Finally, our heartfelt appreciation goes to all of the people who helped with the process of creating and editing this book: Luis Conte, Pam Herzog, Sue Campbell, Joe and Susan Rust. Thank you for sharing your wisdom and perspective.

Lindsay Rust & Steve Campbell
Dancing Drum
Santa Barbara, California, 2010

DISCOVER WEST AFRICA THROUGH MUSIC

Culture can be defined as a collection of human expressions - music, visual art, dance, theater, values, and language - shared by a group of people through the course of history. In traditional societies, like much of West Africa, these expressions overlap and co-exist in daily life. The music and dance work together, the dancers and musicians wear artful costumes, the traditional ceremony has a theatrical quality, and the values, language, and history of the culture permeate every expression. The traditional culture is not complete without each of these parts. Removing one would be like erasing a color from the rainbow.

> *Our goal is to give students a well-rounded experience of the arts, beginning with music, and connecting to a variety of other core content areas including visual arts, language arts, dance, social studies and history.*

This publication is designed as an integrated cultural arts program for schools that will bring a variety of disciplines together in a unified, standards-based curriculum. Our goal is to give students a well-rounded experience of the arts, beginning with music, and connecting to a variety of other core content areas including visual arts, language arts, dance, social studies and history.

By focusing on West Africa, we can access an enormous wealth of engaging cultural information. The significance of West Africa's contribution to world culture cannot be overestimated. West Africans have influenced the arts in nearly every corner of the earth in one way or another, and we hope that this book provides a new insight into the music and arts of this fascinating region.

How To Use This Publication

Teachers can customize *Drumming Up World Music: West Africa* to meet the curriculum goals of each class and grade level. This program can be adapted to present the most age-appropriate activities based on students' needs and abilities, creating an engaging and meaningful educational experience for all students, grades K-8.

Each country section has the following features:

The Rhythm Hunters & Journal Entries

Through their Journal Entries, the "Rhythm Hunters" provide the narrative thread that ties together the content of *Drumming Up World Music: West Africa*. Students can follow along as the Rhythm Hunters travel through the cities and villages of West Africa, experiencing the local culture, making friends, and learning new things.

Use the Journal Entries as stories to engage your students in background information about each of the music and art activities in the book. Journal Entries are written in the first-person so students can more easily place themselves inside the story with the Rhythm Hunters.

Each entry features Reading Comprehension Questions to reinforce and assess student learning, Key Words to build vocabulary, and Pronunciation Notes to help with sounding out new words.

Key Words

- **New** Key Words are marked in **bold**.
- Key Words that have been *used previously* in the text are *italicized*.
- All Key Words are defined in the Glossary at the end of this book.

Pronunciation Notes

Challenging words are sounded out in the margins with pronunciation notes in italics. In cases where we hear commonly used English words within the pronunciation of foreign words, we utilize the English word to make pronunciation easier. For example, the word for "foreigner", **toubab**, has its pronunciation notated as *(two-bob)*. Though the notes are not exact, we've done our best to approximate the sounds of the words in a way that will be effective for elementary students. For more help with pronunciation, use the Pronunciation Guide with audio examples on the

DVD that accompanies this book.

COUNTRY FACT SHEET

Each focus area features a Country Fact Sheet with information about the geography, languages, history, and culture of the country. To give students a deeper understanding of the area of study, read and discuss the Country Fact Sheets as part of your classroom's introduction to the music and art activities. By presenting these pages, you can cover standards for geography, social studies, and history.

LANGUAGES

All of the five focus countries in this book use French as their official language. France controlled the government, economy, and society of much of West Africa from the mid-1600's until 1960, during a historic period known as "colonialism." Senegal, Guinea, Mali, Niger, and Burkina Faso were French "colonies." Since then, people in these countries learned to speak French in addition to their local, African languages. Other countries in West Africa, like Ghana and Nigeria, were colonized by the British and use English as their official language.

Even though the colonial era ended decades ago, these countries still use the languages of their colonizers. However, the local African languages are often more widely spoken and understood.

Linguists estimate that around 2,000 distinct languages are spoken in Africa, making for an incredibly diverse continent. This book provides some simple greetings and vocabulary for 6 African languages.

ETHNIC GROUPS

At least 20 different ethnic groups are mentioned in this book. Members of an ethnic group share a common language, culture, history, and a general geographic location. During the colonial era, when Europeans drew country boundaries, the homelands of many ethnic groups were divided between two or three separate countries. This explains why, for example,

A Woodabe man in Niger

Hausas live in both Niger and Nigeria, and *Malinkés* live in both Mali and Guinea. In reality, much of the music in this book would be played in more than one country because ethnic groups in Africa are not constrained by country boundaries.

THE MUSIC

Drumming Up World Music: West Africa features one drum arrangement and one xylophone arrangement per country. The drum arrangements can be presented with 1-4 levels of difficulty, and the xylophone arrangements have 1-5 levels of difficulty. A variety of time signatures are covered in this book: 4/4, 4/4 swing, 3/4, and 6/8. For a more thorough introduction to the music, read the "About the Music" chapter, starting on page 74.

VISUAL ART ACTIVITIES

Each country features a new visual art activity: *Paper Bead Necklace* (Senegal), *Djembefola Hat* (Guinea), *Dogon Kanaga Mask* (Mali), *Woodabe Pouch* (Niger), and *Bwa Hawk Mask* (Burkina Faso). These visual art activities can be used to create costumes for a student performance, for a student art exhibit, or just for fun.

Each activity has full, step-by-step instructions with illustrations. The level of difficulty ranges from Easy to Advanced. We realize that most music classrooms aren't set up for visual art activities, however music teachers can use these projects in partnership with the art teacher or a classroom teacher to create cross-program connections. Please note that we recommend prepping (pre-cutting) the paper sizes listed in the materials box for each activity.

DVD

In addition to video clips of the drumming and xylophone parts, the DVD that accompanies this book contains some great video footage of Dancing Drum's travels in West Africa. These videos enrich the content of the Travel Journals and give students a more well-rounded perspective on life in Africa. The DVD includes footage of a Bamako wedding party, instructions for learning the Didadi Dance, making a Cross of Agadez, playing the *gasu* calabash drum and the *kalangou* talking drum, spending a day in an African village, and more. We have also included instructions for the visual art activities, which teachers can project while students make their own art projects.

The CD that accompanies this book contains audio examples of all of the Learning Levels: Levels 1-4 for the drum arrangements, and Levels 1-5 for the xylophone arrangements, as well as the drum break and break ending for each song. This CD is designed as a play-along resource for teachers and students. Track numbers are listed at the end of this book, on page 242. You can also reference the track numbers at the top of music notation and rhythm phonics pages.

Lindsay with friends in Larba Birno, Niger

CURRICULUM CONNECTIONS

Drumming Up World Music: West Africa is designed to fulfill a wide range of state and national standards for education. The numbers of the national standards covered by each reading and art activity are noted on the first page of the activity. Music standards covered by the drum and xylophone arrangements are noted on page 79. As you make your way through the program, refer back to the list below for a more comprehensive description of each standard.

Music standards covered by the drum and xylophone arrangements are noted on page 79.

Music

Grades K-4

NA-M.K-4.1
Content Standard #1: Singing, alone and with others, a varied repertoire of music

Achievement Standards covered:
-Students sing from memory a varied repertoire of songs representing genres and styles from diverse cultures
-Students sing ostinati

NA-M.K-4.2
Content Standard #2: Performing on instruments, alone and with others, a varied repertoire of music

Achievement Standards covered:
-Students perform on pitch, in rhythm, with appropriate dynamics and timbre, and maintain a steady tempo
-Students perform easy rhythmic, melodic, and chordal patterns accurately and independently on rhythmic, melodic, and harmonic classroom instruments
-Students perform expressively a varied repertoire of music representing diverse genres and styles
-Students echo short rhythms and melodic patterns
-Students perform in groups, blending instrumental timbres, matching dynamic levels, and responding to the cues of a conductor
-Students perform independent instrumental parts (e.g., simple rhythmic or melodic ostinati, contrasting rhythmic lines, harmonic progressions, and chords) while other students sing or play contrasting parts

NA-M.K-4.3
Content Standard #3: Improvising melodies, variations, and accompaniments

Achievement Standards covered:
-Students improvise "answers" in the same style to given rhythmic and melodic phrases
-Students improvise simple rhythmic and melodic ostinato accompaniments
-Students improvise simple rhythmic variations and simple melodic embellishments on familiar melodies

> *"To participate fully in a diverse, global society, students must understand their own historical and cultural heritage and those of others within their communities and beyond. Because music is a basic expression of human culture, every student should have access to a balanced, comprehensive, and sequential program of study in music."*
> - National Standards for Arts Education (K-4)

From *National Standards for Arts Education*. Copyright © 1994 by Music Educators National Conference (MENC). Used by permission.

The complete National Arts Standards and additional materials relating to the Standards are available from **MENC: The National Association for Music Education,** 1806 Robert Fulton Drive, Reston, VA 20191; www.menc.org

NA-M.K-4.5
Content Standard #5: Reading and notating music

Achievement Standards covered:
-Students read whole, half, dotted half, quarter, and eighth notes and rests in 3/4, and 4/4 meter signatures
-Students use a system (that is, syllables, numbers, or letters) to read simple pitch notation in the treble clef in major keys
-Students identify symbols and traditional terms referring to dynamics and tempo and interpret them correctly when performing

NA-M.K-4.6
Content Standard #6: Listening to, analyzing, and describing music

Achievement Standards covered:
-Students demonstrate perceptual skills by moving, by answering questions about, and by describing aural examples of music of various styles representing diverse cultures
-Students identify the sounds of a variety of instruments, including many orchestra and band instruments, and instruments from various cultures, as well as children's voices and male and female adult voices

NA-M.K-4.8
Content Standard #8: Understanding relationships between music, the other arts, and disciplines outside the arts

Achievement Standards covered:
-Students identify ways in which the principles and subject matter of other disciplines taught in the school are interrelated with those of music (e.g., foreign languages: singing songs in various languages; mathematics: mathematical basis of values of notes, rests, and time signatures; science: vibration of strings, drum heads, or air columns generating sounds used in music; geography: songs associated with various countries or regions)

NA-M.K-4.9
Content Standard #9: Understanding music in relation to history and culture

Achievement Standards covered:
-Students identify by genre or style aural examples of music from various historical periods and cultures
-Students describe in simple terms how elements of music are used in music examples from various cultures of the world
-Students identify and describe roles of musicians (e.g., orchestra conductor, folksinger, church organist) in various music settings and cultures

Grades 5-8

NA-M.5-8.1
Content Standard #1: Singing, alone and with others, a varied repertoire of music

Achievement Standards covered:
-Students sing music representing diverse genres and cultures, with expression appropriate for the work being performed
-Students sing music written in two and three parts

NA-M.5-8.2
Content Standard #2: Performing on instruments, alone and with others, a varied repertoire of music

Achievement Standards covered:
-Students perform on at least one instrument (e.g., band or orchestra instrument, keyboard instrument, fretted instrument, electronic instrument) accurately and independently, alone and in small and large ensembles, with good posture, good playing position, and good breath, bow, or stick control
-Students perform with expression and technical accuracy on at least one string, wind, percussion, or classroom instrument a repertoire of instrumental literature with a level of difficulty of 2, on a scale of 1 to 6
-Students perform music representing diverse genres and cultures, with expression appropriate for the work being performed
-Students who participate in an instrumental ensemble or class perform with expression and technical accuracy a varied repertoire of instrumental literature with a level of difficulty of 3, on a scale of 1 to 6, including some solos performed from memory

> *"Broad experience with a variety of music is necessary if students are to make informed musical judgments. Similarly, this breadth of background enables them to begin to understand the connections and relationships between music and other disciplines. By understanding the cultural and historical forces that shape social attitudes and behaviors, students are better prepared to live and work in communities that are increasingly multicultural. "*
> *- National Standards for Arts Education (5-8)*

NA-M.5-8.3
Content Standard #3: Improvising melodies, variations, and accompaniments

Achievement Standards covered:
-Students improvise simple harmonic accompaniments
-Students improvise melodic embellishments and simple rhythmic and melodic variations on given pentatonic melodies and melodies in major keys
-Students improvise short melodies, unaccompanied and over given rhythmic accompaniments, each in a consistent style, meter, and tonality

NA-M.5-8.5
Content Standard #5: Reading and notating music

Achievement Standards covered:
- Students read whole, half, quarter, eighth, and dotted notes and rests in 3/4, 4/4, and 6/8 and alla breve meter signatures
- Students read at sight simple melodies in both the treble and bass clefs
- Students identify and define standard notation symbols for pitch, rhythm, dynamics, tempo, articulation, and expression
- Students who participate in a choral or instrumental ensemble or class sight-read, accurately and expressively, music with a level of difficulty of 2, on a scale of 1 to 6

NA-M.5-8.6
Content Standard #6: Listening to, analyzing, and describing music

Achievement Standards covered:
-Students describe specific music events (e.g., entry of oboe, change of meter, return of refrain) in a given aural example, using appropriate terminology
-Students analyze the uses of elements of music in aural examples representing diverse

genres and cultures
-Students demonstrate knowledge of the basic principles of meter, rhythm, tonality, intervals, chords, and harmonic progressions in their analyses of music

NA-M.5-8.8
Content Standard #8: Understanding relationships between music, the other arts, and disciplines outside the arts

Achievement Standards covered:
-Students compare in two or more arts how the characteristic materials of each art (that is, sound in music, visual stimuli in visual arts, movement in dance, human interrelationships in theatre) can be used to transform similar events, scenes, emotions, or ideas into works of art
-Students describe ways in which the principles and subject matter of other disciplines taught in the school are interrelated with those of music (e.g., language arts: issues to be considered in setting texts to music; mathematics: frequency ratios of intervals; sciences: the human hearing process and hazards to hearing; social studies: historical and social events and movements chronicled in or influenced by musical works)

NA-M.5-8.9
Content Standard #9: Understanding music in relation to history and culture

Achievement Standards covered:
-Students describe distinguishing characteristics of representative music genres and styles from a variety of cultures
-Students compare, in several cultures of the world, functions music serves, roles of musicians (e.g., lead guitarist in a rock band, composer of jingles for commercials, singer in Peking opera), and conditions under which music is typically performed

VISUAL ARTS

Grades K-4

NA-VA.K-4.1
Content Standard #1: Understanding and applying media, techniques, and processes

Achievement Standards covered:
-Students know the differences between materials, techniques, and processes
-Students use different media, techniques, and processes to communicate ideas, experiences, and stories

NA-VA.K-4.2
Content Standard #2: Using knowledge of structures and functions

Achievement Standards covered:
-Students know the differences among visual characteristics and purposes of art in order to convey ideas
-Students use visual structures and functions of art to communicate ideas

NA-VA.K-4.3
Content Standard #3: Choosing and evaluating a range of subject matter, symbols, and ideas

"Through examination of their own work and that of other people, times, and places, students learn to unravel the essence of artwork and to appraise its purpose and value. Through these efforts, students begin to understand the meaning and impact of the visual world in which they live."

- National Standards for Arts Education (K-4)

Achievement Standards covered:
-Students explore and understand prospective content for works of art
-Students select and use subject matter, symbols, and ideas to communicate meaning

NA-VA.K-4.4
Content Standard #4: Understanding the visual arts in relation to history and cultures

Achievement Standards covered:
-Students know that the visual arts have both a history and specific relationships to various cultures
-Students identify specific works of art as belonging to particular cultures, times, and places
-Students demonstrate how history, culture, and the visual arts can influence each other in making and studying works of art

NA-VA.K-4.5
Content Standard #5: Reflecting upon and assessing the characteristics and merits of their work and the work of others

Achievement Standards covered:
-Students understand there are various purposes for creating works of visual art
-Students describe how people's experiences influence the development of specific artworks

NA-VA.K-4.6
Content Standard #6: Making connections between visual arts and other disciplines

Achievement Standards covered:
-Students understand and use similarities and differences between characteristics of the visual arts and other arts disciplines
-Students identify connections between the visual arts and other disciplines in the curriculum

VISUAL ARTS
Grades 5-8

NA-VA.5-8.3
Content Standard #3: Choosing and evaluating a range of subject matter, symbols, and ideas

Achievement Standards covered:
-Students integrate visual, spatial, and temporal concepts with content to communicate intended meaning in their artworks
-Students use subjects, themes, and symbols that demonstrate knowledge of contexts, values, and aesthetics that communicate intended meaning in artworks

> *"Study of historical and cultural contexts gives students insights into the role played by the visual arts in human achievement.*
> *As they consider examples of visual art works within historical contexts, students gain a deeper appreciation of their own values, of the values of other people, and the connection of the visual arts to universal human needs, values, and beliefs."*
> - National Standards for Arts Education (5-8)

NA-VA.5-8.4
Content Standard #4: Understanding the visual arts in relation to history and cultures
Achievement Standards covered:
-Students know and compare the characteristics of artworks in various eras and cultures
-Students describe and place a variety of art objects in historical and cultural contexts
-Students analyze, describe, and demonstrate how factors of time and place (such as climate,

resources, ideas, and technology) influence visual characteristics that give meaning and value to a work of art

NA-VA.5-8.5
Content Standard #5: Reflecting upon and assessing the characteristics and merits of their work and the work of others
Achievement Standards covered:
-Students compare multiple purposes for creating works of art
-Students analyze contemporary and historic meanings in specific artworks through cultural and aesthetic inquiry
-Students describe and compare a variety of individual responses to their own artworks and to artworks from various eras and cultures

NA-VA.5-8.6
Content Standard #6: Making connections between visual arts and other disciplines
Achievement Standards covered:
-Students compare the characteristics of works in two or more art forms that share similar subject matter, historical periods, or cultural context
-Students describe ways in which the principles and subject matter of other disciplines taught in the school are interrelated with the visual arts

Grades K-4

NA-D.K-4.1
Content Standard #1: Identifying and demonstrating movement elements and skills in performing dance
Achievement Standards covered:
-Students demonstrate the ability to define and maintain personal space
-Students demonstrate accuracy in moving to a musical beat and responding to changes in tempo
-Students demonstrate kinesthetic awareness, concentration, and focus in performing movement skills
-Students attentively observe and accurately describe the action (such as skip, gallop) and movement elements (such as levels, directions) in a brief movement study

> *"Through dance education, students can come to an understanding of their own culture and begin to respect dance as a part of the heritage of many cultures. As they learn and share dances from around the globe, as well as from their own communities, children gain skills and knowledge that will help them participate in a diverse society."*
>
> - National Standards for Arts Education (K-4)

NA-D.K-4.5
Content Standard #5: Demonstrating and understanding dance in various cultures and historical periods
Achievement Standards covered:
-Students perform folk dances from various cultures with competence and confidence
-Students learn and effectively share a dance from a resource in their own community; describe the cultural and/or historical context
-Students accurately answer questions about dance in a particular culture and time period (for example: In colonial America, why and in what settings did people dance? What did the dances look like?)

 **DANCE**

Grades 5-8

NA-D.5-8.1
Content Standard #1: Identifying and demonstrating movement elements and skills in performing dance

> *Achievement Standards covered:*
> -Students demonstrate the following movement skills and explain the underlying principles: alignment, balance, initiation of movement, articulation of isolated body parts, weight shift, elevation and landing
> -Students accurately transfer a spatial pattern from the visual to the kinesthetic
> -Students accurately transfer a rhythmic pattern from the aural to the kinesthetic
> -Students identify and clearly demonstrate a range of dynamics / movement qualities
> -Students demonstrate increasing kinesthetic awareness, concentration, and focus in performing movement skills
> -Students demonstrate accurate memorization and reproduction of movement sequences
> -Students describe the action and movement elements observed in a dance, using appropriate movement/dance vocabulary

> *"The study of dance provides a unique and valuable insight into the culture or period from which it has come. Informed by social and cultural experiences, movement concepts, and dance-making processes, students integrate dance with other art forms."*
>
> - *National Standards for Arts Education (5-8)*

NA-D.5-8.3
Content Standard #3: Understanding dance as a way to create and communicate meaning

> *Achievement Standards covered:*
> -Students demonstrate and/or explain how costuming can contribute to the meaning of a dance

NA-D.5-8.5
Content Standard #5: Demonstrating and understanding dance in various cultures and historical periods

> *Achievement Standards covered:*
> -Students competently perform folk and/or classical dances from various cultures; describe similarities and differences in steps and movement styles
> -Students learn from resources in their own community (such as people, books, videos) a folk dance of a different culture or a social dance of a different time period and the cultural/historical context of that dance, effectively sharing the dance and its context with their peers
> -Students accurately describe the role of dance in at least two different cultures or time periods

SOCIAL STUDIES & HISTORY
GEOGRAPHY (K-12)

NSS-G.K-12.1
The World in Spatial Terms

Achievement Standards covered:
- Understand how to use maps and other geographic representations, tools, and technologies to acquire, process, and report information from a spatial perspective.
- Understand how to analyze the spatial organization of people, places, and environments on Earth's surface.

NSS-G.K-12.2
Places and Regions

Achievement Standards covered:
- Understand the physical and human characteristics of places.

NSS-G.K-12.3
Physical Systems

Achievement Standards covered:
- Understand the characteristics and spatial distribution of ecosystems on Earth's surface.

NSS-G.K-12.4
Human Systems

Achievement Standards covered:
- Understand the characteristics, distribution, and migration of human populations on Earth's surface.
- Understand the characteristics, distribution, and complexity of Earth's cultural mosaics.
- Understand the patterns and networks of economic interdependence on Earth's surface.
- Understand the processes, patterns, and functions of human settlement.
- Understand how the forces of cooperation and conflict among people influence the division and control of Earth's surface.

NSS-G.K-12.5
Environment and Society

Achievement Standards covered:
- Understand how physical systems affect human systems.
- Understand the changes that occur in the meaning, use, distribution, and importance of resources.

WORLD HISTORY (5-12)

NSS-WH.5-12.5
ERA 5: Intensified Hemispheric Interactions, 1000-1500 CE

Achievement Standards covered:
- the growth of states, towns, and trade in Sub-Saharan Africa between the 11th and 15th centuries.

LANGUAGE ARTS
ENGLISH (K-12)

NL-ENG.K-12.1
Reading for Perspective

Achievement Standards covered:
-Students read a wide range of print and nonprint texts to build an understanding of texts, of themselves, and of the cultures of the United States and the world; to acquire new information; to respond to the needs and demands of society and the workplace; and for personal fulfillment. Among these texts are fiction and nonfiction, classic and contemporary works.

NL-ENG.K-12.3
Evaluation Strategies

Achievement Standards covered:
-Students apply a wide range of strategies to comprehend, interpret, evaluate, and appreciate texts. They draw on their prior experience, their interactions with other readers and writers, their knowledge of word meaning and of other texts, their word identification strategies, and their understanding of textual features (e.g., sound-letter correspondence, sentence structure, context, graphics).

NL-ENG.K-12.9
Multicultural Understanding

Achievement Standards covered:
-Students develop an understanding of and respect for diversity in language use, patterns, and dialects across cultures, ethnic groups, geographic regions, and social roles.

STANDARDS

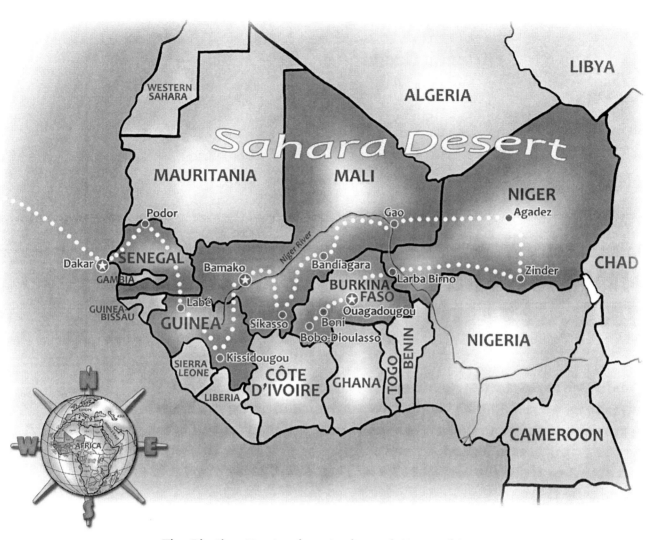

The Rhythm Hunters' route through West Africa

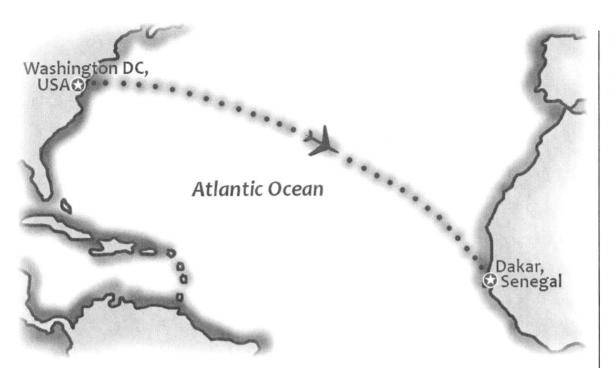

STANDARDS:
NA-M.K-4.9
NA-M.5-8.8 & 9
NSS-G.K-12.2
NL-ENG.K-12.9

Journal Entry #1

SOMEWHERE OVER THE ATLANTIC: THE RHYTHM HUNTERS

Finally, we're on our way to Africa! After months of planning our adventure, we're flying 35,000 feet above the Atlantic Ocean. We're nervous and excited to find out what the next few months will bring, and we can't wait to step foot on African soil for the first time. After reading and studying about the continent for so long, it will be wonderful to actually *be* there.

People tend to think that Africa is so far away. Actually, the trip isn't very long. We departed this morning from Washington, D.C., and will land in Senegal's capital city, Dakar, 8 hours later.

Right now, we can look out the airplane window and see the blue Atlantic Ocean stretching for miles in every direction. It looks like an endless sea, but we know that on the other side, the massive continent of Africa waits for us. Did you know that Africa has over 50 countries? Over 2,000 languages are spoken there. The continent is divided into 5 regions: West Africa, North Africa, East Africa, Central Africa, and Southern Africa. Since it's such a huge place, we'll only be able to cover 5 countries in West Africa before we have to go back home: Senegal, Guinea, Mali, Niger, and Burkina Faso.

Senegal (*say-nay-gall*)
Guinea (*geh-knee*)
Mali (*mah-lee*)
Niger (*knee-zhair*)
Burkina Faso
(*Bur-key-nah Fah-so*)

We call ourselves "The Rhythm Hunters" because we'll be on a musical **safari**, traveling through cities, villages, forests, deserts, and **savannas** to discover the rhythms of West Africa. During our trip, we will be seeking out teachers who can show us the rhythms and songs played in their villages, and talk to us about the music that pulses through their everyday lives. We want to learn everything we can about the drums and all of the other **unique** instruments that come from West Africa.

Africa is sometimes called "The Motherland" because it's where our earliest **ancestors** walked the earth, and it's likely where we discovered our ability to make music. For as long as anyone can recall, people in Africa have played drums for music and used drumming to communicate messages. Some **researchers** even believe that our ability to speak developed alongside the first drums. It's clear that, from the earliest times, music has played an important role in Africa.

We wonder what our first day in Africa will be like...Will it be hot? What will the food taste like? Will people be friendly? How will we travel from town to town, and where will we sleep? How will we find our teachers?

There's so much we still have to learn, and we're sure that Africa has many surprises in store for us!

Comprehension Questions:

1) Fill in the blank: Africa has over _____ countries.

2) Name the 5 regions of Africa.

3) Name 5 countries in West Africa.

4) Why is Africa sometimes called "The Motherland"?

5) *Fill in the blank:* In Africa, drums are used to play music and to _____.

The First Humans
DNA technology has enabled scientists to trace the first humans (**homo sapiens**) to an area in East Africa known as the *Great Rift Valley*. Though there is still a great deal of debate about our human origins, science points to the first human ancestors originating in Africa.

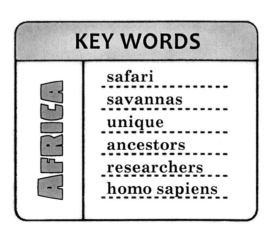

KEY WORDS

AFRICA

safari

savannas

unique

ancestors

researchers

homo sapiens

STANDARDS:
NSS-G.K-12.1
NSS-G.K-12.3

A **mile** is a unit of length used to measure **distances**. One mile is equal to 5,280 feet.

A **square mile (mi²)** is a unit used to measure **area**. The size of a square mile is equal to a four-sided figure measuring one mile on each side, or 5,280 x 5,280 feet. The total surface area of one mi² is equal to 27,878,400 square feet.

5,280 feet (1 mile)

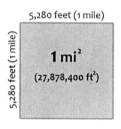

1 mi²

(27,878,400 ft²)

"The Lower 48" are the **contiguous** states of the USA, not including Alaska and Hawaii.

Fact Sheet

HOW BIG IS AFRICA?

Africa is the world's second largest continent, with a land area of 11.7 million square miles (mi²). It has 61 countries and territories, and a population of over 1 billion people. The Sahara Desert, which stretches across the northern third of Africa, from the Atlantic Ocean to the Red Sea, covers 3.63 million mi². West Africa, which includes the countries of Benin, Burkina Faso, Côte D'Ivoire, Gambia, Ghana, Guinea, Guinea-Bissau, Liberia, Mali, Mauritania, Niger, Nigeria, Senegal, Sierra Leone, and Togo, stretches across 3.11 million mi². Niger is the largest country in West Africa, with an area of 489,000 mi². Gambia is West Africa's smallest country, with only 4,360 mi² in surface area, and only 30 miles wide at its widest point.

In comparison, the size of the lower 48 states of the USA is 3.12 million mi². The country of Canada measures 3.85 million mi². The continent of Europe contains 47 countries and measures 3.93 million mi². Asia, the world's largest continent, measures 17.21 million mi², and its largest country, Russia, has a land area 6.59 million mi².

Comprehension Questions:

1) How does the size of your country compare to the region of West Africa?

2) How does the size of your country compare to West Africa's largest country, Niger?

3) How many times would the lower 48 states of the United States fit into the continent of Africa?

4) How many times would West Africa's smallest country, The Gambia, fit into your country?

5) Find out the size of your home state. How many times would it fit into the continent of Africa?

traveler walking behind a camel on a street in Niamey, Niger

TRAVEL JOURNALS

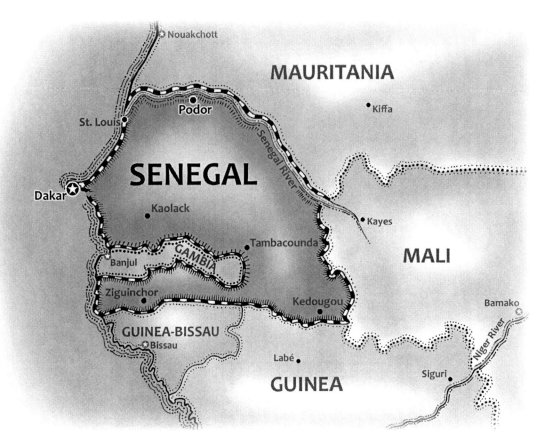

Fact Sheet

SENEGAL

Senegal occupies the western most part of the African continent, and it is the closest departure point to the Americas. The shape of the country is unusual because it almost completely surrounds another country called Gambia, which is located in southern Senegal around the Gambia River.

The **Senegalese** have a rich culture of music that includes traditional styles, as well as modern *Afropop*, and a style of dance music called **mbalax**, based on the rhythms of *sabar* drums.

Senegal has three distinct geographical areas:

Learn to speak Wolof!
(A language from Senegal)

WOLOF	ENGLISH
Asalam·alekum. (*a-sah-lam a-lay-koom*)	Hello.
Nanga def? (*nan-gah deaf*)	How are you?
Mangi fii rekk. (*ma-nyee fah-rek*)	I am fine.
Jerejef! (*jair-uh-jef*)	Thank you!
Baal ma. (*ball-mah*)	Please.

STANDARDS:
NSS-G.K-12.1, 2, 3, 4, 5
NL-ENG.K-12.9

VITAL STATISTICS

Official Name:
République du Senegal

Capital: Dakar

Area: 76,062 mi²

Population: 11.1 mil.

Currency: CFA franc

Official Language: French

Ethnic Groups:
Wolof, Fulani, Toucouleur, Serer, Lebou, Jola

Senegal (*seh-neh-gall*)

Wolof (*wool-off*)

Senegalese (*say-nay-gall-eez*) a person or thing from Senegal

mbalax (*mm-bah-lah*)

sabar (*sah-bar*) The next section covers sabar drums.

The flag of Senegal

FAMOUS MUSICIANS FROM SENEGAL:
Youssou N'Dour
Baaba Maal
Mansour Sek
Doudou Ndiaye Rose
Cheikh Lô

Serer (sair-air)

Fulani (foo-lawn-ee)

Did you know
Senegal's first president, *Léopold Sénar Senghor*, was also a poet? He personally wrote the Senegalese national anthem, called *"Pincez tous vos koras, frappez les balafons."*

In English, this translates to *"Everyone strum your koras, strike the balafons."*

A **kora** is a type of harp played in West Africa, and a **balafon** is an African xylophone.

THE WEST

Western Senegal is home to beautiful, sandy beaches and seaside villages. Many people here make a living through fishing. Senegalese fishermen paint their boats in bright colors and paddle out to the ocean to net their daily catch of fish. Western Senegal is inhabited mostly by *Wolof* and *Serer* people.

THE NORTH AND EAST

Senegal's northern and eastern zones are drier than Western Senegal, and receive a smaller amount of rainfall per year. This area is nearer to the **Sahara** Desert. Many people Northern and Eastern Senegal, especially the *Fulani*, make their living by raising **livestock** – sheep, goats, and cows. Others farm crops including corn and peanuts. People who live close to one of Senegal's northern rivers can fish and grow rice for a living.

THE SOUTH

The southernmost region of Senegal, the Casamance, features lush, **tropical** forests and white sand beaches. It is populated mostly by the *Jola* people. Though this region is a popular destination for tourists, most people in southern Senegal region make their living through fishing and growing rice.

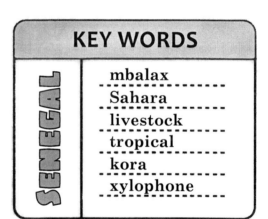

KEY WORDS

SENEGAL

mbalax
Sahara
livestock
tropical
kora
xylophone

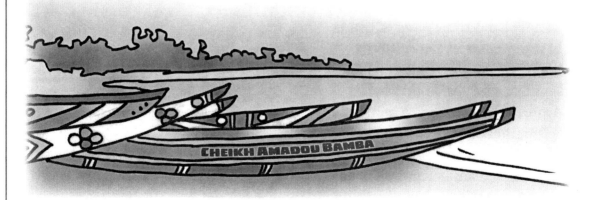

Senegalese fishing boats

STANDARDS:
NA-M.K-4.8, 9
NA-M.5-8.9
NL-ENG.K-12.9

Journal Entry #2: Dakar
LIFE IN THE CAPITAL CITY

SENEGAL

Our final descent. We glide down through the clouds, swooping in an arc along the coast of Senegal, and cruise down the runway for a smooth landing. Our flight attendant opens the airplane door and a blast of warm air washes over everyone in the plane. At last, we're in Africa!

After getting our **passports** stamped by the airport officers, we head out to the curb to meet our friend Mabiba, who will be helping us during our stay in Dakar.

"Nanga def?" we hear from across the busy roadside. It's Mabiba, shouting a greeting in **Wolof** at us. She's waiting by her car with her son Djibo.

"Magni farek!" we respond in unison. We are so happy to see a familiar face in this foreign land. Everyone smiles and hugs. Before we realize what's happened, our bags are in the trunk of Mabiba's car and we're driving into downtown Dakar.

"Our first stop is Sandaga Market," Mabiba says. "We need to buy some ingredients for dinner. I am going to cook Chicken *Yassa* for you!"

"That sounds delicious!" we say, feeling hungry after our long flight.

We arrive at the market, and at the entrance we pass through a sea of bead **merchants** who call to us from behind their piles of beads in every color of the rainbow. We buy a couple of strands for Mabiba, and she is thrilled! Around the corner is a woman selling bunches of bananas, sweet potatoes, melons, and onions. She smiles and asks us to buy something. Mabiba finds the ingredients she needs for the

Market woman selling fruits and vegetables

Dakar *(dah-car)*

Wolof *(wool-off)* is the most widely spoken language in Senegal. It is also the name of a large ethnic group.

A QUICK WOLOF LESSON:

Nanga def? *(nan-gah deaf)* How are you?

Magni farek! *(ma-nyee fah-rek)* Just fine!

Sandaga Market is Dakar's biggest marketplace.

Yassa is a classic Senegalese sauce that combines elements of French and African cuisine. Made with lemons, dijon mustard, and onions, the sauce can be served with chicken, fish, or vegetables. See page 34 for an authentic recipe for Senegalese Yassa.

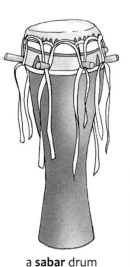

a **sabar** drum

N'Daaga (en-dah-gah)

Sabar (sah-bar) is a very popular style of drumming and dance created by Wolof people in Senegal. Named for a type of drum, sabar rhythms are used to play both traditional and modern musical styles.

Yassa - lemons, onions, garlic, and ginger - and pays the woman.

Suddenly, from a distance, we hear the sound of drumming. It thunders through the marketplace and calls us closer. At the edge of the market, in the shade of palm tree, we see three men with Wolof **sabar** drums playing a joyful, galloping rhythm. They strike their drums with a stick in one hand and with the palm of their other hand. The stick makes a high cracking sound, and the hand makes a deep, bass boom.

We step closer to the drummers, and they motion for us to stay. As we watch and listen, we notice that each of them is playing a different pattern. The drummers are creating a **polyrhythm**, with many layers of **rhythm** weaving together to make beautiful music.

Mabiba says, "This is the *N'Daaga* rhythm. It's one of the first rhythms that many *Senegalese* children learn to dance to."

A crowd draws around the drummers, and a dancer bursts into the middle of the circle, arms and legs flying in a display of physical strength and grace. Her movements match the powerful rhythms of the sabar drummers, and for the first time in Africa we see how drumming and dancing inspire each other. Afterwards, we have a chance to talk with the drummers, and they teach us how to play the N'Daaga rhythm.

Comprehension Questions:

1) Who stamps the travelers' passports?

2) What kind of food did Mabiba plan to cook?

3) What kinds of things can you find at Dakar's Sandaga Market?

4) What kind of drums do the travelers see at the market?

5) What rhythm did the drummers play?

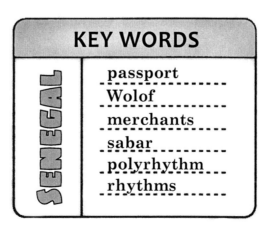

KEY WORDS

SENEGAL

passport
Wolof
merchants
sabar
polyrhythm
rhythms

Recipe
YASSA

Yassa is a *traditional* style of sauce cooked in Senegal that combines elements of African and French food. It can be made with fish, chicken, and/or vegetables. *(If you are making a vegetarian sauce, skip the first step and double the quantity of vegetables.)*

INGREDIENTS

Meat:
¼ cup peanut oil
2 lb meat *(1 chicken cut into pieces or 4-6 fillets of firm white fish)*
Salt and pepper

Spice paste:
1 T whole peppercorns
1-2 cubes bouillon *(chicken, fish, or veggie flavor)*
½-1 inch fresh ginger, peeled and sliced
4 garlic cloves, chopped

Sauce ingredients:
2 large onions, halved and thinly sliced
2 large carrots, peeled and cut into chunks
2 medium yellow potatoes, halved and sliced with skin on
juice of 5-6 lemons
1-2 lemons sliced in thin rounds, rind on
10 green olives *(no pimentos)*
3-4 cups water or stock
1/2 cup or more Dijon mustard
habanero pepper sauce *(optional)*
jasmine rice *(cooked)*

SENEGAL

COOKING INSTRUCTIONS

STEP 1:

Heat a large, deep pan over medium heat. Add peanut oil, and carefully lay in the pieces of meat. Salt and pepper. Sauté the meat until it's lightly brown on both sides and remove from pan. Cover meat and set aside.

STEP 2:

In the drippings oil, add sliced onions and stir. Prepare spice mixture, grinding peppercorns first, then garlic and ginger, then bouillon cubes. Add spice paste to sautéing onions and stir. When onions are soft and transparent, add carrots and onions and cook for a minute, stirring gently.

STEP 3:

Add broth. Stir. Add Dijon mustard and lemon juice. Stir well to combine. If you're making the sauce with chicken, add the chicken pieces now, and then float olives and lemon slices on top. Cover and reduce heat. Cook at a low simmer for 30 minutes. Add water if sauce is too thick. If you're making the sauce with fish, add the cooked fish pieces in the last 5 minutes of simmering so that they don't fall apart in the stew. Yassa should be a thinner sauce, but not watery.

STEP 4:

Check to adjust seasonings. Serve hot over jasmine rice with habanero pepper sauce on the side.

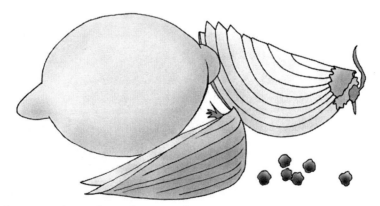

3 important ingredients for Yassa: lemon, onion, and black peppercorns

STANDARDS:
NA-M.K-4.9
NA-M.5-8.9
NSS-G.K-12.2
NL-ENG.K-12.9

Journal Entry #3: Podor
SONG OF THE RIVER

SENEGAL

The next day, we travel from the capital city, *Dakar*, to the north of Senegal and a vibrant town called *Podor*. This is the home village of two famous *Senegalese* musicians, Baaba Maal and Mansour Sek. We've come here hoping to learn more about the music of this town which has inspired such great talents.

Podor *(poe-door)*

The Senegal River runs right by Podor. It's the center of activity for the village, and it's the first place we visit on today's rhythm hunting adventure. On the river bank, we meet a friendly fisherman who offers to take us on a boat ride. It's a hot day, and being out on the water sounds fantastic, so we board his boat and push away from the shore.

His boat is shaped like a long, pointed canoe with a flat bottom. In this part of the world, it's called a **pirogue**. While we're moving close to the river banks, our guide propels the boat forward by pushing a pole against the river bottom. When we reach deeper water, he uses a paddle to move the boat. The water is peaceful, and we have time to relax and think about the adventure ahead. Huge flocks of birds pass overhead, and fish leap from the water as our boat passes by.

a pirogue on the river

As the fisherman rows, his paddle bumps against the side of the wooden boat.

A **pirogue** *(pea-row-guh)* is a type of boat common throughout West Africa, used mainly for river travel.

The river water rushes alongside with each stroke and creates a natural *rhythm* of *bump-swish-rest-bump-swish-rest*. Our guide begins to sing along to the rhythm of the river: *"Kokoriko, Miyaabele ko-o-o!"*

We are captivated by his beautiful song, and when he finishes singing, we ask him about it.

"This song is called *Miyaabele*," he says. "It's a **folk song** from the **Fulani** people of Podor."

"What do the **lyrics** mean?" we ask.

He responds, *"Kokoriko* is the crow of the rooster, waking the people up. *Miyaabele* encourages Africans to work together to build a better future."

We ask the fisherman if he would teach us the song and **melody** for Miyaabele. He gladly agrees and we stop at a beach along the river to learn this beautiful song.

Comprehension Questions:

1) What two famous Senegalese musicians come from Podor?

2) What river runs by Podor?

3) What natural rhythms do the travelers observe while they're on the Senegal River?

4) What is *Kokoriko*?

5) What is the message of the *Miyaabele* song?

Miyaabele
(mee-ah-bay-lay)

The Fulani
(foo-lawn-ee)
are a diverse group of people, spread throughout every country in West Africa. Some live a **nomadic** lifestyle, herding animals, while others are **sedentary** farmers or fishermen. They all share a common language called *Pular*, or *Fulfulde*.

SENEGAL

KEY WORDS	
SENEGAL	pirogue ....
	folk song ....
	Fulani ....
	nomadic ....
	sedentary ......
	lyrics ....
	melody ....

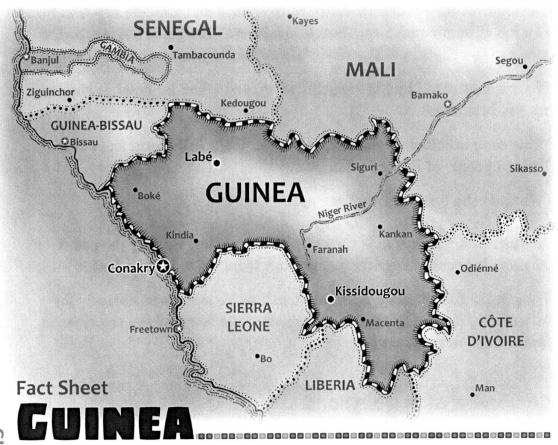

STANDARDS:
NA-M.5-8.8 & 9
NSS-G.K-12.1, 2, 3, 4, 5
NL-ENG.K-12.9

VITAL STATISTICS

Official Name: République de Guinée

Capital: Conakry

Area: 94,981 mi²

Population: 10.1 mil.

Currency: Guinean franc

Official Language: French

Ethnic Groups: Fulani, Malinké, Susu, Landoma

Guinea (geh-knee)

Conakry (con-ah-kree)

Pular is the language spoken by Fulani people in Guinea.

Guinean (geh-nay-yan) a person or thing from Guinea.

Les Ballets Africains (lay bal-aze ah-free-kan)

Ballet is the French word for dance.

Fact Sheet
GUINEA

Not to be confused with Guinea-Bissau, Equatorial Guinea, or Papua New Guinea, the country of *Guinea*, West Africa, is sometimes called "Guinea-Conakry" to distinguish it from other countries with similar names.

The people of Guinea are proud of their **diversity**, and over 20 distinct **ethnic groups** call Guinea home. In Guinea, the *Fulani* people are the most numerous. Some of the other groups that live in Guinea are the *Malinké, Susu, Kissi,* and *Landoma*.

Guinean music and culture has spread far and wide. A **choreographer** from Guinea, Keita Fodeba, created Africa's first touring drum and dance **ensemble**, called *Les Ballets Africains* which has performed on the

Learn to speak Pular!
(A language from Guinea)

PULAR	ENGLISH
On jaraama. (ohn jah-rah-mah)	Hello.
Hida e jam? (hee-dah ee jahm)	How are you?
Jam tun. (jahm toon)	I am fine.
A jaraama! (ah jah-rah-mah)	Thank you!
En ontuma. (En own-too-mah)	See you later.

The flag of Guinea

Fouta Djallon
(foo-tah jah-lon)

FAMOUS MUSICIANS FROM GUINEA:
Bembeya Jazz
Mamady Keita
Sekouba Bambino
Mory Kanté

Niger *(knee-zhair)*
Senegal *(seh-neh-gall)*
Gambia *(gam-bee-ya)*

Côte d'Ivoire *(coat dee-vwar)*

Malinké *(mah-lin-kay)*

Liberia *(lye-bier-ee-ah)*

Sierra Leone *(see-air-ah lee-own)*

world's biggest stages since the 1950s. For many years, beginning with Guinea's first president Sekou Toure in the 1960s, the government invested heavily in supporting the *traditional* arts and artists of Guinea.

Guinea has four distinct geographic areas:

FOUTA DJALLON, OR MID-GUINEA

Guinea's most impressive natural feature is a mountainous area called the *Fouta Djallon*, which runs from the north to the south of the country. These mountains are the source of many of West Africa's most important waterways; the *Niger* River, the *Senegal* River, and the *Gambia* River all begin in the Fouta Djallon. For this reason, Guinea is sometimes called the "water tower" of West Africa. The Fulani people consider the Fouta Djallon their **homeland**.

One of many waterfalls in the Fouta Djallon

LOW GUINEA

Low Guinea covers the coastal area, bordered by the Atlantic Ocean to the west and the Fouta Djallon to the east. Hot and humid hill country, Low Guinea is inhabited mostly by people of the Susu ethnic group, who make their living through fishing and farming.

UPPER GUINEA

Upper Guinea is high and dry. Located in the eastern part of the country, this area borders the countries of *Mali*, Senegal, and *Côte d'Ivoire*. Its spacious **plateaus** and grassy plains are populated mostly by the *Malinké* people.

FORESTED GUINEA

Forested Guinea covers the southern region and shares borders with the countries of *Liberia* and *Sierra Leone*. This mountainous area is filled with small rivers, dense jungles, and swamps. Many different ethnic groups live here.

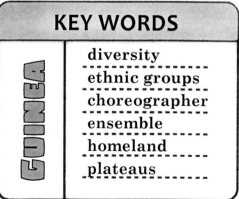

KEY WORDS

GUINEA

diversity
ethnic groups
choreographer
ensemble
homeland
plateaus

STANDARDS:
NA-M.K-4.9
NA-M.5-8.8
NL-ENG.K-12.9

Journal Entry #4: Labé
BLESSING FROM A DJELI

GUINEA

Our first day in Guinea begins with a lucky encounter. We arrive in the northern town of *Labé* late in the day. A slender man with dark hair, sparkling eyes, and a big smile approaches us.

"*Toubab!*" he says, "*Bienvenue a Labé!* Welcome to Labé."

"*Merci.* Thank you." We both reply with a smile.

Then the man asks, "What brings you to this place?"

"We're here to learn about the music of Guinea," we explain.

"Ah haaaa!" The smiling man says. "Then you are having a lucky day. I am a musician, my parents are musicians, and all of my grandparents before them played music, too. I come from a **djeli** family. Some people would call us **griots**."

We can hardly believe our good luck as the djeli brings out his **balafon** and begins to play us a song. A crowd gathers around as the djeli sings. His song praises the great Kings of the ancient **Mande** empire and tells of the musical talents of his djeli ancestors who played for those kings hundreds of years ago. Then he devotes a few lines of his song to us:

> "*You are from a foreign land, and you do not yet know much about the ways of our people. May your travels in West Africa bring you the knowledge you seek. May you return home to tell the world of the marvelous music of our people, and build bonds of friendship that will cross thousands of miles.*"

djeli (*jeh-lee*)

Djelis, or griots, are the traditional musicians and history-keepers of West Africa. Many can recite long histories from memory. Djelis inherit their musical status through their families.

Labé (*lah-bay*)

toubab = foreigner (*two-bob*)

A Quick French Lesson:

bienvenue = welcome (*bee-en-ven-oo*)

merci = thank you (*mair-see*)

griots (*gree-ohs*)

Mande (*mahn-day*)

a **balafon** from Guinea

The balafon (*bah-lah-fone*) is a West African style of *xylophone*, the ancestor to modern-day **marimbas** played in orchestras all over the world. In Guinea, the balafon is reserved for djelis who play it while singing praise songs honoring the great families and stories of West African history.

See *The Story of the Balafon* on the next page for more about this unique West African instrument.

The crowd cheers and nods in approval, and we have been blessed on our journey.

"Will you teach us more about your music?" we ask the djeli.

He replies with a smile, "Yes! Of course. Tonight is the full moon, and all of the djelis in Labé will come here to play. We will teach you *Lamba, the song of the djeli.*"

The full moon is a time for music and celebration all over Africa. In areas of the world that have few streetlights or electric lamps, the bright light of the full moon invites everyone to gather together outside and make music late into the night.

As the sun sets, the full moon rises, and djeli plays his balafon again. Other djelis begin to arrive with their instruments. Before long, there's a full *ensemble* playing, complete with balafon players, drummers, and shaker players. The djelis teach us Lamba, which is a happy, upbeat song with a strong **swing feel**. Lamba gives thanks for the gift of music and celebrates the important role of the djeli in keeping the musical *traditions* of Guinea alive and well.

As people begin to dance to the Lamba music, we sit back and enjoy this perfect moment under the light of the full moon.

Comprehension Questions:

1) How does the village react to the full moon?

2) What is the name of the African xylophone?

3) What is a djeli?

4) What rhythm do the travelers learn?

5) For what purpose do the djelis play Lamba?

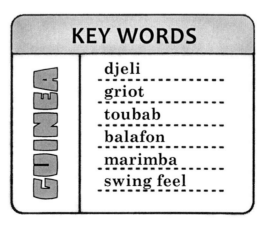

KEY WORDS

GUINEA

djeli

griot

toubab

balafon

marimba

swing feel

Cultural Connections
THE STORY OF THE BALAFON

The *balafon*, or **bala**, is a type of *xylophone* from West Africa. The balafon is made of numerous slats of hardwood cut in different sizes. These create different pitches when played with **mallets**. The slats are tied to a frame made of wood or bamboo, and dried **gourds** are attached underneath each slat. The purpose of the gourds is to increase the volume and sound quality, or **resonance**, of the instrument.

gourds attached to the back of the balafon

The balafon is found in numerous countries in West Africa – Guinea, Burkina Faso, Mali, Côte d'Ivoire, Senegal, Ghana, and Gambia all have balafon traditions. In Guinea, the balafon is the most important instrument for accompanying *djeli* singers. Today, djelis still tell the story of the very first balafon, called the "Susu Bala", which came from the *Susu* people of Guinea.

The story begins in the 13th century, during a dispute between two kings. *Soumaworo Kante*, king of the Susu people, possessed a magic balafon that only he could play. He kept the instrument locked up in the top of a tall building that only he was allowed to enter. Soumaworo said that even if a fly touched the balafon, he would kill it.

This was during a time of war between the Susu kingdom and the *Mande* Empire. The Susu King, Soumaworo Kante, and the Mande King, *Soundiata Keita*, were fighting for control of the same lands. In a battle, Soumaworo's warriors captured a favorite djeli of Soundiata's, and took him back to the Susu King's palace where he was held prisoner.

Balafon is a 2-part word. The first part, *bala-*, refers to the instrument itself. The second part, *-fo*, refers to the act of playing bala. In Africa, the instrument itself is commonly called *"bala."* The term *"balafon"* is more appropriately used as a verb, however it is commonly accepted as the correct name of the instrument.

There are many different types of xylophones from West Africa. Balafons from Guinea generally have 18-21 keys tuned to a C-diatonic scale, just like Orff xylophones.

Soumaworo Kante
(Su-ma-wo-ro Kahn-tay)

Soundiata Keita
(Soun-jah-ta Kay-tah)

Note: There are several different versions of the Balafon Story.

GUINEA

One day, the djeli snuck into the house where the balafon was held, and he began to play the instrument. Soumaworo heard the beautiful sounds and, despite his anger at the djeli for playing the forbidden instrument, the king was amazed that the djeli could play the balafon even better than himself. He then appointed the djeli as guardian of the instrument and gave him the new name of "Bala Fasseke Kouyate" (*"the balafon player"*).

Some time around 1236 A.D., Soundiata's Mande armies conquered Soumaworo's Susu kingdom. They took the magical Susu Balafon and djeli Kouyate back to Mande land. To the delight of King Sundiata, the djeli played magnificent songs on the Susu Balafon. These original songs played by Bala Fasseke Kouyate have been preserved to the present day by djelis in Guinea and Mali.

The original Susu Bala itself still exists. Around 800 years old, it is kept in a village in the north of Guinea. The special instrument is guarded by a djeli family that brings it out only for very special occasions and holidays. It is said that all Mande balafons made today are tuned according to the Susu Bala.

The Susu Balafon has been declared a treasure of humanity by UNESCO.

Comprehension Questions:

1) What materials are balafons made from?

2) The balafon is played in which countries?

3) According to the story recounted above, which kingdom invented the balafon?

4) What happened to the original Susu Balafon?

5) Approximately how old is the original Susu Balafon today?

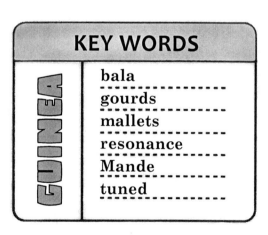

KEY WORDS

GUINEA

bala
- - - - - - - - - - - - - -
gourds
- - - - - - - - - - - - - -
mallets
- - - - - - - - - - - - - -
resonance
- - - - - - - - - - - - - -
Mande
- - - - - - - - - - - - - -
tuned
- - - - - - - - - - - - - -

The Mande Empire - also known as the Mali or Mandeng Empire - was one of the greatest eras of West African history. At its peak, the Mande Empire spanned the areas now known as Mali, Guinea, Senegal, Côte d'Ivoire, Burkina Faso, Gambia, and Niger. The Mande Empire existed from about 1230 to 1600 A.D. West African arts and music flourished during this time, and many of the traditions that began then still thrive today throughout West Africa.

UNESCO is the United Nations Educational, Scientific, and Cultural Organization, devoted to preserving the special histories and cultures of the world.

Art Connection: **Djembefola Hat** (*pg. 202*)

STANDARDS:
NA-M.K-4.8, 9
NA-M.5-8.8, 9
NL-ENG.K-12.3, 9
NSS-G.K-12.4

Journal #5: Kissidougou

ENCOUNTER WITH A DJEMBEFOLA

Our next adventure takes us south into Forested Guinea, to a town called *Kissidougou*, close to the border with Sierra Leone and Liberia.

We arrive in Kissidougou and discover that it's market day. The town has a festive atmosphere and people from all over the region are arriving with goods to sell at the market – bags of rice, bananas and mangoes, sandals, beads, and many other items. The *merchants* flood into the market area and set up their temporary shops under a shady spot.

Weekly markets like this one happen all over West Africa. They are an opportunity for people to meet, catch up on news, conduct business, and buy the things they need for the week.

Along with the merchants, groups of musicians come to entertain people at market day. In the center of Kissidougou's marketplace, a group of young drummers is setting up their instruments, getting ready for their show. There are three **djembe** players and three **dundun** drummers, who each play a bell and a different size of drum. The largest dundun is the **dundunba**, the middle size is called the **sangban**, and the smallest dundun is the **kenkeni**. The biggest drum has the lowest sound and the smallest drum makes the highest sound. The family of three dunduns works together to play the *melodic* bass line of the music.

The drummers' costumes are bright and colorful, and the leader

Kissidougou
(*key-si-du-gu*)

Djembefola
(*jem-bay-fo-lah*)

The djembefola with his hat and djembe drum. Three *ksing-ksing* rattles are attached to the sides of the drum. They create a buzzing sound when the djembe is played.

dundun (*doon-doon*)

Dunduns can also be called *djun-djuns*, *dununs*, or *doons*.

GUINEA

The Dundun Family:
Dundunba, Sangban, & Kenkeni

of the group wears an amazing hat that's so impressive, we ask him, "Can you tell us about your hat?"

The djembe player smiles and responds, "This is a **djembefola** hat. I wear this hat because I am an expert in the art of playing djembe."

We ask, "Are you a djembefola?"

He laughs and says, "Yes! I know almost everything about djembe. More than 100 different *rhythms* and their uses. Here in Guinea, we have rhythms for many different purposes. We drum for weddings, holidays, festivals, funerals, *initiations*, planting, the *harvest*, and all kinds of events in the community. Each of these events has a specific set of rhythms that the djembefola must know how to play."

We are amazed as the djembefola leaps into action, calling his troupe together with a few swift beats on his drum. It's showtime, and the *ensemble* begins their performance for the marketplace. The dundun players set the tempo with a fast *polyrhythm*, and two djembe players play an **accompaniment** rhythm on their drums. The djembefola is the star of the show. He steps to the front and plays a powerful **solo** on his drum, drawing the attention of the crowd. The whole marketplace starts moving to the beat, and we join in the joyful dance!

For a some great examples of **djembe music from Guinea,** listen to any CD by Mamady Keita or Famadou Konate.

djembe
(jem-bay)

Comprehension Questions:

1) What instruments are part of the drum ensemble?

2) What is a djembefola?

3) How many rhythms does the djembefola know?

4) Name five different occasions in Guinea where rhythms are played on drums.

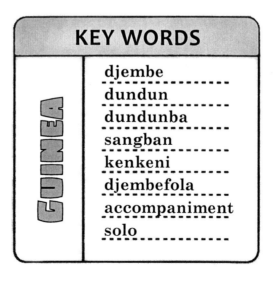

KEY WORDS	
GUINEA	djembe _____
	dundun _____
	dundunba _____
	sangban _____
	kenkeni _____
	djembefola _____
	accompaniment
	solo _____

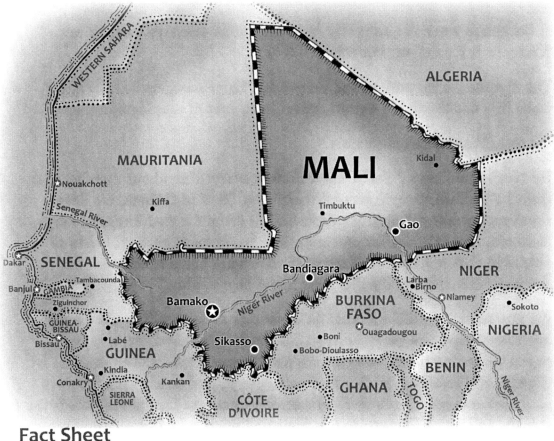

STANDARDS:
NA-M.K-4.8, 9
NA-M.5-8.8, 9
NSS-G.K-12.1, 2, 3, 4, 5
NL-ENG.K-12.9

VITAL STATISTICS

Official Name:
République du Mali

Capital:
Bamako

Area:
478,839 mi²

Population:
14.5 million

Currency:
CFA franc

Official Language:
French

Ethnic Groups:
Bambara, Soninké, Malinké, Fulani, Dogon, Songhai, Tuareg

Mali (*mah-lee*)

French is Mali's official language, but 40 or more African languages are widely spoken in Mali. The most common is **Bambara**, or Bamanankan, which is used for communication by about 80% of Mali's people.

Malian (*mah-lee-an*) is the word used to refer to someone or something from Mali.

Fact Sheet

MALI

Few countries in the world can match Mali's cultural richness. The golden age of Mali's music began during the *Mande* Empire in the 13ᵗʰ century. Musicians of that time were also the historians and storytellers, a tradition that continues in modern Mali through the *djeli*, or *griot*. Today, many djelis in Mali have successfully merged their traditional styles of music with modern music, creating a wonderful new style known as **Afropop**.

Mali is also home to the "Mali Blues" - guitar music with similar *melodies* and *rhythms* as American blues music. Many scholars believe that this Malian music is the *ancestor* of the American blues.

Malians are proud of their

Learn to speak Bambara!
(A language from Mali)

BAMBARA	ENGLISH
A ni sogoma. (*ah knee soh-go-mah*)	Good morning.
I Ka Kene? (*ee kah keh-ney*)	How are you?
Kene. (*keh-ney*)	I am fine.
Aniche! (*ah-knee-chey*)	Thank you!
Kambe soni. (*Kam-bay soh-knee*)	See you later.

The flag of Mali

Tuareg (twa-regh)

FAMOUS MUSICIANS FROM MALI:
Ali Farka Toure
Oumou Sangare
Salif Keita
Habib Koite
Toumani Diabate
Tinariwen

diversity. Over 40 distinct languages are spoken in the country, and Mali's landscape covers 4 different geographical areas:

SAHARAN ZONE

The mighty *Sahara* Desert covers about 65% of Mali's land area. The Sahara stretches across the northeastern part of the county, continuing through the bordering countries of Algeria, Mauritania, and Niger. The desert is home a to colorful *nomadic* group, the *Tuareg*, who are sometimes called the "Blue Men of the Sahara" because of their **indigo** robes and turbans.

SAHELIAN ZONE

Sahel is an *Arabic* word that means "shore", and the Sahelian zone is the shore of the Sahara Desert. In Mali, the Sahel runs in a band across the center of the country. It is a transition zone between the dry desert and the

KEY WORDS	
MALI	Afropop
	Bambara
	indigo
	Sahelian
	Sudanese
	cultivating

greener areas in the southwest of Mali. This area is inhabited by many different peoples – *Songhai, Dogon, Fulani, Bambara,* and others. Most people in the Sahel make a living by farming.

SUDANESE ZONE

The southwestern part of Mali is much greener than the rest of the country because it receives more rainfall every season. This area, called the **Sudanese** Zone, shares a border with the countries of Guinea, Côte D'Ivoire, Senegal, and Burkina Faso. The *Malinké,* Bambara, and Senufo people call this area home, and most make a living as farmers.

NIGER RIVER

Niger (knee-zhair)

Did you know
that the name of Mali translates to "hippopotamus" in the Bambara language? Another animal can be found in the name of Mali's capital city, Bamako, which means "crocodile river" in Bambara. Both crocodiles and hippos live in and around the Niger River today.

Africa's 3rd largest river, the Niger, flows through the heart of Mali. People who live along the Niger River – the Boso, Sorko, and Songhai – depend on the water for nearly everything. Activities like fishing, **cultivating** rice, and *trading* up and down the waterways are the center of their daily lives.

Hippos in the Niger River

STANDARDS:
NA-M.K-4.8, 9
NA-M.5-8.8, 9
NL-ENG.K-12.3, 9

Journal Entry #6: Bamako

A WEDDING IN THE CITY

MALI

Our first stop in Mali is the sprawling capital city, *Bamako*. This is one of West Africa's largest cities, with over a million people. The Niger River runs right through the heart of Bamako, and houses made of mud and cement line both banks of the river. On some days, you may have a chance to see a crocodile in the river. That's where the name Bamako comes from; it means "Crocodile River" in the local language, *Bambara*.

Bamako (bah-mah-ko)

Today is a lucky day because we have been invited to attend the wedding of a friend in downtown Bamako. We put on our best clothes and arrive at noon. The women of the wedding party are dressed in colorful, flowing gowns, headscarves in every color of the rainbow, and sparkling jewelry. Everyone is excited and looking forward to the festivities that surround a wedding in Mali – drumming, dancing, singing, and great food.

The wedding party is set up under a tent in the middle of the street. Plastic chairs line the edges of the tent, and on one end, a drum *ensemble* has begun to play an exciting *rhythm* on *djembes*, *dunduns*, and **konkoni** drums. A group of women arrives in bright blue costumes, and they begin to sing into a **megaphone.** Their songs praise the families that are joined in marriage today. The singers are *jelis*, or *griots*, the historian singers of Bamako.

Djembe (jem-bay)
Dundun (doon-doon)
Konkoni (kon-kon-ee)

Djelis (jeh-lees)
Griots (gree-ohts)

Djelis and drummers at a wedding party in Bamako. The drummer on the left is playing a konkoni drum.

As they sing the family history, members of the family line up to shower the singers with money, some sticking 1000 **CFA** bills to their foreheads.

As the money flows, the energy of the singers and drummers increases, and soon everyone in the entire tent is up and dancing in a huge circle. A djembe **soloist** steps into the middle of the circle and is met by a young dancer who leaps in the air, braids flying and feet pounding to the beat of his drum. As soon as she exits, another dancer takes center stage, and the djembe soloist tunes into her movements, **accenting** each step with a drum beat. Next, it's the drummer's turn to dance, and he does a flip in the air and lands in the splits, to the great delight of the circle of women in the tent. Everyone is smiling!

At one point, we catch a quick glimpse of the bride, who slips by nearly unnoticed since she is surrounded by her sisters, aunts, female cousins, and mother. It's unlikely that we'll see the bride or the groom dance today, but there are plenty of other people who are ready to take part in the music. The wedding party lasts all day and into the night, shifting between the singing of the djelis, the drumming of the *djembefolas*, and the dancing of family and friends. It's a wedding celebration that we will remember forever.

Comprehension Questions:

1) What does the name Bamako mean?

2) Where is the wedding party set up?

3) Who entertains the wedding party?

4) What is the job of the djelis?

5) What types of drums are played at the wedding party?

A common way to thank a djeli in West Africa is by sticking money bills to his or her forehead.

A common currency in French-speaking countries in West Africa is the **CFA**, or West African franc. 1000 CFA is equal to about 2 US dollars.

Djembefola
(jem-bay-fo-lah)

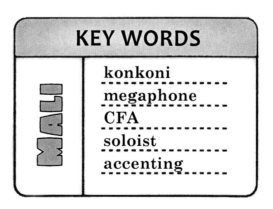

KEY WORDS

MALI

konkoni

megaphone

CFA

soloist

accenting

Music Connection: **Didadi** *(pg.130)*
DVD Connection: **Didadi Dance**

STANDARDS:
NA-M.K-4.8, 9
NA-M.5-8.8, 9
NL-ENG.K-12.3, 9

DIDADI DANCE
STANDARDS:
NA-D.K-4.1, 5
NA-D.5-8.1, 5

Journal Entry #7: Sikasso

THE WASSOULOU SOUND OF THE SOUTH

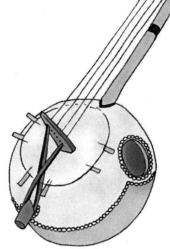

Kamele N'Goni: the Youths' Harp

Our next stop in Mali is the city of *Sikasso*. This area is the homeland of some great music known as the **Wassoulou** Sound. The name Wassoulou refers to an area in southern Mali, in the Wassoulou river valley, inhabited by a mix of *Bambara* and *Fulani* people. The music from this area has become famous around the world through *Afropop* stars like Oumou Sangare and Rokia Traore.

We arrive in Sikasso and go straight to the local radio station, where we have an appointment with DJ Djeliba to learn more about the great music of this area. We're in luck because DJ Djeliba is featuring a Wassoulou band live on the radio today, and she has invited us into the studio to watch.

The Wassoulou band is set up and playing when we arrive. The drummers play *djembes* and *dunduns*, and a percussionist keeps time by scraping a **kariyan**. In addition, there are two **string** players, one on electric guitar and the other on **kamele n'goni**, a type of harp from Mali. Together, the strings and **percussionists** support the powerful vocals of the Wassoulou singer. We listen closely and are captivated by the *unique* sound.

During a commercial break, we have a chance to ask DJ Djeliba about Wassoulou music and what makes it special. We discover that it has a different function than much of the music that we've encountered so far in West Africa.

Sikasso
(see-kas-so)

Wassoulou
(Waa-sou-lou)

For a wonderful example of Wassoulou music, listen to **Oumou Sangare's** 1989 CD release, *Moussoulou (Women)*.

kariyan
(ka-ree-yan)

MALI

"First of all," Djeliba says, "In Wassoulou music, anyone with the desire to sing, dance, or play an instrument is welcome to do so. Djelis must be born into musical families, but Wassoulou performers are musicians by choice, not by birth."

She continues, "Another unique thing about Wassoulou music is its message. Most Wassoulou singers are women, and their songs often address issues like women's rights, modern families, and marriage. In contrast, djeli singers speak mainly of ancient stories from the past and family histories."

"So, would you say that the younger generation are the biggest fans of Wassoulou music?" we ask.

"Yes! Definitely," says Djeliba. "The youth of Mali appreciate the modern messages of Wassoulou music, and they love the *Didadi* rhythm that makes the music sound so good. Listen...The band is going to play a song called *Didadi* next."

The commercial break ends and we're back on the air with the Wassoulou band. The kamele n'goni begins to play, and all of the other instruments layer in one-by-one. The last layer of sound is the Wassoulou singer, her powerful voice broadcasting over the airwaves of Sikasso. After their performance, the Wassoulou band teaches us a *traditional* Didadi rhythm and song.

Comprehension Questions:

1) What instruments make up the Wassoulou band?

2) What topics are commonly discussed in Wassoulou music?

3) How are Wassoulou performers different from djelis?

4) Why does Wassoulou music appeal to the younger generation?

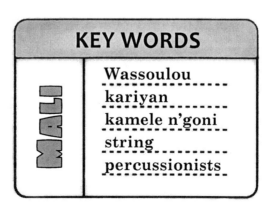

KEY WORDS

MALI

Wassoulou

kariyan

kamele n'goni

string

percussionists

STANDARDS:
NA-M.K-4.8, 9
NA-M.5-8.8, 9
NL-ENG.K-12.3, 9
NA-VA.K-4.4, 5, 6
NA-VA.5-8.4, 5, 6
NSS-G.K-12.2
NA-D.5-8.3

Journal Entry #8: Bandiagara Plateau
THE MYSTERIOUS DOGON

Our next adventure takes us into the heart of Mali – *Dogon* country. The Dogon people are known for their *unique tradition* of masks. For hundreds of years, they have inhabited an area of cliffs in the central part of Mali, called the *Bandiagara Plateau*. For this trip, we need to hire a guide who can take us to the **remote** and hidden places of Dogon country. We're grateful to find Mamadou, a friendly and trustworthy man with years of experience climbing the cliffs and finding the special parts of this interesting area.

Dogon houses on the side of a cliff

Bandiagara
(*bahn-jah-gah-rah*)

Dogon (*doe-gone*)

We depart for our adventure in Dogon country early in the morning. Traveling by car, and then on foot, Mamadou fills us in on the history of the Dogon. He explains, "The Dogon people first came to this area centuries ago from the western part of Mali because they wanted to escape invaders that threatened their way of life. The Bandiagara cliffs were in a far away place, and they felt safe here. People called the Tellem lived here before the Dogon, and they built houses very high up in the cliffs. The Dogon saw this and built their houses into the cliffs, too. Look, you can see one of the first Dogon houses there!"

We look up and see a cluster of rectangular houses made of reddish clay, each one a little different. They look like they are made by an artist, with decorations shaped in the clay, some of them painted red, black, yellow, and white. Each house has its own **granary** topped with a roof of grass that looks like a pointy hat. As we walk around the houses built into the cliffs, we notice that the nicest buildings have wooden doors carved with scenes of people, animals, and plants.

Colors have different meanings for the Dogon. Black stands for "water," red for "fire," white for "air," and yellow for "earth."

A **granary** is a place where people store their grain.

MALI

Anthropologist
Marcel Griaule
recorded the names
of over **80 different
rhythms** played
for Dogon mask
performances.

Kanaga Mask
(kah-nah-gah)

bullroarer
an oval board on a
string, spun over
one's head to make a
howling sound.

As the sun begins to set, we hear the first sounds of drums from a nearby village. Mamadou smiles and says that we're lucky to be here on this day, because the Dogon are about to perform a traditional mask dance to honor the life of a village elder who recently passed away. As we approach the sound of the drums, a group of dancers on stilts passes us by. Another group wearing masks of animals – monkeys, antelopes, snakes, and birds – dances towards the music.

We reach the drummers just in time to see the arrival of the *Kanaga* masks, the Dogon **symbol** of the universe. As the crowd grows, each of the masks moves around the **ceremony** area in a way that tells its story through dance. Mamadou explains, "To the Dogon, masks represent everything important in the world. The performance of masks brings to life the *ancestors*, the animals, the plants, and the people of the Dogon." The masked dancers weave around the circle, driven by the *rhythms* of the drums. The festivities continue late into the night, and suddenly fall silent with the **eerie** howl of a **bullroarer**. This sound signals the end of the ceremony, and everyone walks home quietly into the mysterious, dark night.

Comprehension Questions:

1) Why did the Dogon people first come to the Bandiagara Plateau?

2) What do the Dogon houses look like?

3) What kind of masks do the travelers see?

4) How do the masks tell their story?

5) What is the purpose of the mask dance that the travelers witness?

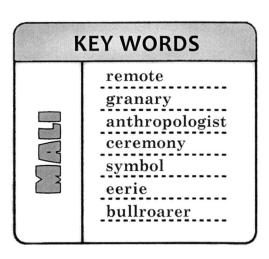

KEY WORDS

MALI

remote

granary

anthropologist

ceremony

symbol

eerie

bullroarer

MALI

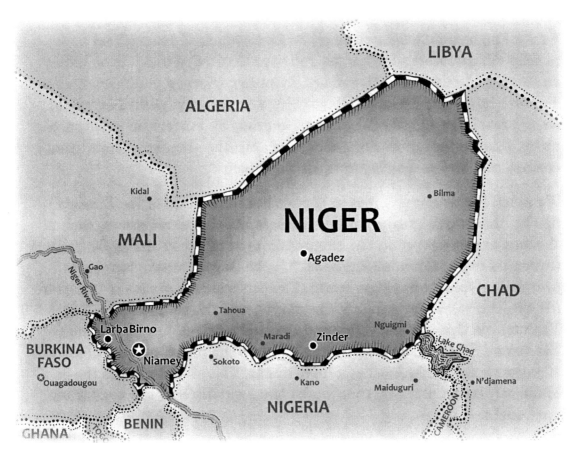

VITAL STATISTICS

Official Name: République du Niger

Capital: Niamey

Area: 490,350 mi²

Population: 15.9 mil.

Currency: CFA franc

Official Language: French

Ethnic Groups: Hausa, Zarma, Songhai, Fulani, Tuareg, Kanuri

Niger *(knee-zhair)*

Tuaregs *(twa-rehgs)*

Nigerien *(knee-zhair-ee-en)* is the word used to refer to someone or something from Niger.

Fact Sheet
NIGER

Niger is West Africa's largest country by land area. Over 20 languages are spoken in this *diverse* and peace-loving country. From the *turban-wearing Tuaregs* that live in the desert north to the *Songhai* fishermen that live on the banks of the Niger River, each of Niger's people has a history and *culture* that makes them *unique*.

Niger inhabits the boundary between the *Arabic* cultures of North Africa and the African peoples that live south of the Sahara. Both influences can be heard in **Nigerien** music.

Learn to speak Songhai-Zarma!
(A language from Niger)

ZARMA	ENGLISH
Fofo. *(foe-foe)*	Hello.
Mate ni go? *(mah-tay knee go)*	How are you?
Bani samey. *(bah-knee sah-may)*	I am fine.
Fonda goy! *(fon-dah goy)*	Thank you!
Kala tonton. *(kah-lah ton-ton)*	See you later.

FAMOUS MUSICIANS FROM NIGER:
Mamar Kassey
Yacouba Moumouni
Mali Yaro
Etran Finatawa

tenere *(ten-eh-ray)*

Aïr Massif
(ah-ear mas-seef)

acacia *(ah-kay-sha)*
baobab *(bah-oh-bob)*

Did you know that Niger is home to one of West Africa's last remaining herds of giraffes? Their population has been threatened for many years, however it has recently begun to recover through the efforts of wildlife **conservation** groups.

Niger is home to 4 distinct geographic regions:

DESERT NORTH

The massive *Sahara*, or "**tenere**", covers the northern part of Niger. Most of this area is flat land with little to no water or trees for miles around. Some of the desert has rolling dunes of white sand. In the few places where water comes to the surface, one can find an **oasis** of ponds and palm trees, a welcome resting place for people traveling across the dry Sahara. Niger's desert north also features a low mountain chain called the *Aïr Massif*.

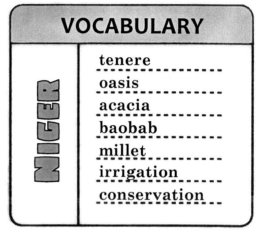

NIGER	VOCABULARY
	tenere
	oasis
	acacia
	baobab
	millet
	irrigation
	conservation

SAHELIAN ZONE

Most of southern Niger is in the Sahelian Zone. *Sahel* is an Arabic word that means "edge" or "shore", and the Sahel is the shore of the Sahara. This area is characterized by dry, flat lands dotted with trees like the **acacia** and **baobab,** which have *adapted* to live in the *arid climate*. In most years, the Sahel receives enough rainfall for farmers to crow crops of **millet** and peanuts. This area is inhabited by many different peoples – *Zarma, Hausa,* and *Fulani,* among others.

NIGER RIVER & SOUTHWEST NIGER

Africa's 3rd largest river, the Niger, flows through the western portion of the country. People who live along the Niger River – the *Songhai* and Zarma – depend on the waterway for life. The Niger River is used for food production - fishing, *cultivating* rice, **irrigation**, watering *livestock* - and for transportation by boat. Most of the land along the river and in the deep southwest corner of Niger is green and lush, in contrast to the dry Sahel and desert areas nearby.

Giraffes in Niger

STANDARDS:
NA-M.K-4.8, 9
NA-M.5-8.8, 9
NSS-G.K-12.2, 3, 4, 5
NSS-WH.5-12.5
NL-ENG.K-12.3, 9

Journal Entry #9: The Route from Gao to Agadez
A CAMEL CARAVAN

NIGER

Moussa, our Tuareg guide through the desert, with his camel and turban

To reach our next destination, we decide to travel like the locals do, and ride camels deeper into the *Sahara*. We hire a guide and a couple of camels, and follow an old **caravan** route from *Gao*, Mali, to the desert city of *Agadez*, in the north of Niger. This trail has been traveled for many hundreds of years as a *trade* route.

In the old days, when the trade of salt and gold was big business, *Tuaregs* ran frequent caravans between the salt mines of the Sahara, north of Agadez, and the Niger River at Gao. Upon crossing the desert with their salt and reaching the river, they could transfer their goods to boats and ship them to the coast, then return to the desert for another trading mission. The old trade routes still exist today, and you can still experience what it's like to caravan from the Niger River into the Sahara on the back of a camel.

The camels that we ride are perfectly **adapted** to living in the desert, with tall, skinny legs to keep them away from the heat of the sand, long eyelashes to keep sun and sand out of their eyes, and a camel hump that stores extra fat and water for long desert crossings. Like the nomads who still travel these lands on their camels, we adapt to the desert climate by wrapping **turbans** around our heads. Turbans protect us from the sun, sand, dry air, and high temperatures of the Sahara.

We ride all day through a flat, **desolate** landscape dotted with scrubby thorn bushes. In the morning, we pass a family of *Woodabe* people herding their cattle. They have a unique, artistic way of dressing themselves, and they are very proud of their beauty. In the afternoon,

Did you know that in the 1800s, some camel caravans were so large that they stretched for more than 15 miles from beginning to end and included more than 10,000 camels?

The Sahara used to have many rivers, lakes and animals before climate change turned it into desert. Ancient rock art found north of Agadez depicts animals like giraffes, lions, fish, and buffalo that can't survive in the desert environment of today.

A **turban** is a cloth that people wrap around their heads to protect them from the sun and dryness of the desert.

Woodabe
(woh-dah-bay)

calabash, or **gasu**
(kah-lah-bash) (gah-sue)

mollo
(mow-low)

we spot what look like white mountains on the horizon. As we ride closer, we see that the mountains are actually huge sand dunes, sculpted into waves and valleys by powerful desert winds. As the sun sets, we find a place to camp in a green *oasis* at the foot of the dunes. We water the camels, fill up our water jugs, and cook dinner over a campfire. The stars are twinkling and bright in this place so far from city lights.

For the next several days, we continue on our trip through the desert toward Agadez. One night, we camp next to a family of Tuaregs who invite us to share dinner with them. We eat a porridge of *millet* with sweet dates and goat cheese, and finish with three rounds of sweet tea. It's delicious after a long day in the desert.

After dinner, our hosts turn their **calabash** bowls into drums, which they call **gasu**. They play a beat that feels like the *rhythm* of a camel galloping through the desert. One person plays a *melody* on a **mollo** – a type of guitar with three strings – and a lady begins to sing. The rest of the group follows her lead, swaying their arms to the rhythm of the song. "Time to dance the *Takamba!*" our hosts say, and everyone joins in the graceful, flowing dance, smiles flashing brightly around the fire. Later, our new friends teach us the Takamba rhythm and song.

Comprehension Questions:

1) What old caravan route do the travelers cross?

2) What were some of the important items of trade for camel caravans?

3) What adaptations do camels have for living in the desert?

4) What do the adventurers eat when they are invited to have dinner with the Tuaregs?

5) What instruments do the Tuaregs play after dinner?

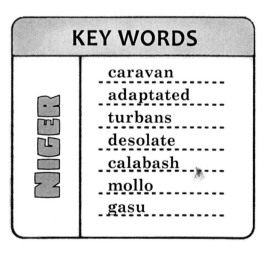

KEY WORDS

NIGER

caravan
adapted
turbans
desolate
calabash
mollo
gasu

STANDARDS:
NA-VA.K-4.4, 6
NA-VA.5-8.4, 6
NL-ENG.K-12.3, 9

Cultural Connections
TIFINAGH: THE TUAREG ALPHABET

Cross of Agadez
a Tuareg symbol made by
silversmiths, signed in Tifinagh

Tifinagh (*tif-in-agh*)

Tamashek
(*tah-mah-sheck*)

The Cross of Agadez
is a well-known
symbol of the Tuareg
people and their
capital city, Agadez.
Though the exact
meaning of the cross
is a matter of debate,
some Tuaregs say
that the circle at
the center of the
cross symbolizes a
well and the smaller
circles around it are
the footprints of
desert jackals that
come to drink at the
well.

The *Tuareg* people of the *Sahara* are one of the few groups in Africa to have developed their own style of writing. Called *Tifinagh*, the script was originally used to keep court records and write poetry in *Tamashek*, the language of the Tuaregs.

No one knows the exact history of Tifinagh, but there is evidence of this writing style from almost 2,000 years ago. Several different versions of Tifinagh are used by Tuareg people throughout West and North Africa.

These days, Tuareg children are taught to write in Tifinagh by their parents and teachers, who often instruct the youngsters by tracing letters in the sand.

All true Tuareg
crosses are signed on
the back in Tifinagh
with the name of
the silversmith who
crafted the cross.

On the facing page is a chart of the Tifinagh alphabet, with letter sounds in English.

Can you figure out how to write your name in Tifinagh*? For example, the girl's name "Belkisa" would be written like this:

$$\ominus \div \| \therefore \lessgtr \odot \cdot$$

One difficulty of
writing in Tifinagh is
that it's missing one
of the letters that we
use in English: O

* Go to the DVD for a projectable image of the Tifinagh alphabet.

NIGER

Tifinagh Alphabet

A	·	N	|
B	⊖	P	ჽ
C	Ɔ	Q	···
D	∨	R	○
E	÷	S	⊙
F	Ⅱ	T	+
G	⋈	U	:
H	⋮	V	△
I	⋛	W	⊔
J	I	X	::
K	∴	Y	≶
L	‖	Z	ⵣ
M	⊏		

STANDARDS:
NA-M.K-4.8, 9
NA-M.5-8.8, 9
NSS-G.K-12.2, 4
NL-ENG.K-12.3, 9

Zinder *(zin-dair)*

Journal Entry #10: Zinder
THE CALL OF THE KALANGOU

Adamou playing his kalangou

Our next adventure takes us to a **Hausa** city in the south of Niger called *Zinder*. Our drummer friend, Adamou, is expecting us there.

After hours on a bus, we finally reach our destination and are happy to see Adamou waiting for us at the bus stop. He smiles and says, "*Sannu da zuwa!* Welcome!" We spend a few moments exchanging the traditional greetings in Hausa, asking questions like "How is your family?" "How is your work?" To all of these questions, the response is always "*Lafiya lo!*" or, "In health!"

"Ah!" says Adamou, "We have to go quickly. I have a surprise for you. Today we are playing for the **Sultan** of Zinder!" Adamou is always full of surprises. We toss our bags into his car and drive into the city, where we'll see the Hausa "King" of Zinder.

In a few minutes, we are standing in the courtyard of the Sultan's palace with Adamou and his troupe of drummers. Adamou picks up his **kalangou** and calls the group to attention with a couple of swift taps on the drum. The kalangou is known outside of Africa as a "**talking drum**" because the drummer can change the pitch of the drum by squeezing its sides while playing. This creates a "talking" effect, where the drummer can **imitate** speech. Drummers who have been playing kalangou for a long time can actually communicate with each other on their drums just the same as speaking.

Hausa *(how-sah)* is the most widely spoken language in West Africa, with over 24 million native speakers. The majority of Hausa people live in the countries of Niger and Nigeria.

"Sannu da zuwa!" *(sah-new dah zoo-wah)* means "Welcome!" in Hausa.

The Sultan of Zinder is a *traditional* position of power that has existed since the 1700s. The sultan acts as a regional king, and he can make legal decisions that affect the people of his kingdom.

NIGER

kalangou
(kah-lan-gou)

There are many variations on the **kalangou drum** throughout West Africa. In Senegal, the Wolof people call it "*tama*," in Ghana, the Akan people call it "*dondo*," and the Bambara people of Mali it "*toumani*."

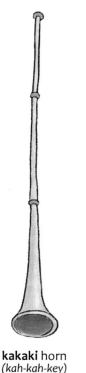

kakaki horn
(kah-kah-key)

When the music heats up, a group of magnificent horses rides into the palace compound. They are decorated in beautiful silver and leather harnesses. Their riders are equally impressive, wearing long robes called **boubous** in bright colors of red, yellow, and green, topped with red *turbans*. Adamou explains, "These are the guards of the Sultan. Behind them is the Sultan."

The drummers accelerate the *rhythm* for the arrival of the Sultan, and he arrives on his horse amid thunderous drumming and the high-pitched call of the **kakaki** horn. His flowing robe, called a grand **boubou,** and his white turban blow in the breeze. The Sultan looks larger than life as he dismounts from his horse and strides into his palace, confident in his role as the most powerful person in the city. The guards of the Sultan line up in front of the palace door, and Adamou leads the drummers into a loud **crescendo**. The music ends with a drum roll and a big boom, and the drummers' job is done for the day.

Comprehension Questions:

1) How are the travelers greeted by their friend Adamou?

2) What is the response to the Hausa greetings?

3) How does the kalangou imitate speech?

4) How are the guards of the Sultan dressed?

5) What is the function of the Sultan?

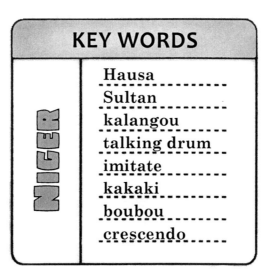

KEY WORDS	
NIGER	Hausa
	Sultan
	kalangou
	talking drum
	imitate
	kakaki
	boubou
	crescendo

STANDARDS:
NA-M.K-4.8, 9
NA-M.5-8.8, 9
NSS-G.K-12.3
NL-ENG.K-12.3, 9

Journal Entry #11: Larba Birno
THE RHYTHMS OF VILLAGE LIFE

drumming and dancing in Larba Birno

Our next stop is a village in the far west of Niger called *Larba Birno*. This is a really special place. We spent lots of time here the last time we visited West Africa, and the people of Larba Birno are like old friends to us.

We arrive at the **chief's** compound in the late afternoon, and the village erupts with excitement. Our smiling friends surround us and say, *"Fonda kayan!* Welcome!" Tonight, we'll rest and catch up with the chief's family around the dinner fire. Tomorrow, we'll walk through the village, meeting and greeting everyone we can.

In the morning, the first sound we hear is a rooster. He starts a little weakly, and after his vocal chords warm up, he can really crow! Soon, we hear another sound – the wooden pounding of a **mortar and pestle** as a woman grinds grain for the morning meal. Next, we hear the squeaking wheels of a donkey cart passing by, the hooves of the donkey clomping along in a *rhythm*. In the distance, we can hear the first buckets of water sloshing from the well. Little birds twitter from a tree. It seems like the whole village wakes up together in a song.

As the day warms up, we walk around the village, greeting our friends. The back and forth rhythm of our words creates its own song that we repeat over and over again during the day. *"Ni kani bani?* Did you sleep in health?" they ask. We respond, *"Bani samey.* Only health." We ask, *"Mate hu borey?* How's your family?" and they respond, *"Bani samey."* It's considered polite throughout West Africa to take your time and properly greet people by asking about their family, their health, their

Larba Birno
(lar-bah bier-noh)

"Fonda kayan!"
(fon-dah kai-yan)
is Songhai-Zarma for "Welcome!"

A quick **Songhai-Zarma** lesson:

Ni kani bani?
(knee-ka-knee bah-knee)
Did you sleep well?

Bani samey.
(Bah-knee saa-may)
Only health.

Mate hu borey?
(mah-tay hoo bor-ay)
How's your family?

NIGER

doundoun drum

business, and life in general before moving on to any other discussion.

At last, we reach our friend Udu's house. He's been waiting for us and preparing a tea *ceremony* to welcome us back to the village. We smile and chat as we sit together on the cool, sand floor of his brick house and share three rounds of tea. Udu pours the tea from a small silver teapot in a long arc, without splashing a drop. The first round of tea is strong and bitter, the second round is weaker and a little sweet, and the third round of tea is very sweet, almost like a melted piece of candy.

In the late afternoon, as the day begins to cool, a **quartet** of drummers arrives with their *kalangou* and **doumdoum** drums. They play a dance rhythm, and the beat calls people from their homes. Soon, there's a circle of dancers around the drummers, and people are taking turns in the middle of the circle, showing off their best dance moves. The dance party continues on into the night, and we are so happy to celebrate with our friends.

NIGER

Tea with Udu

Comprehension Questions:

1) What are some of the sounds that the travelers hear in the morning?

2) How do people greet each other in West Africa?

3) How many rounds of tea do the travelers drink with Udu?

4) What happens when the drummers start to play?

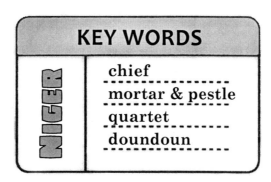

KEY WORDS

NIGER

chief
mortar & pestle
quartet
doundoun

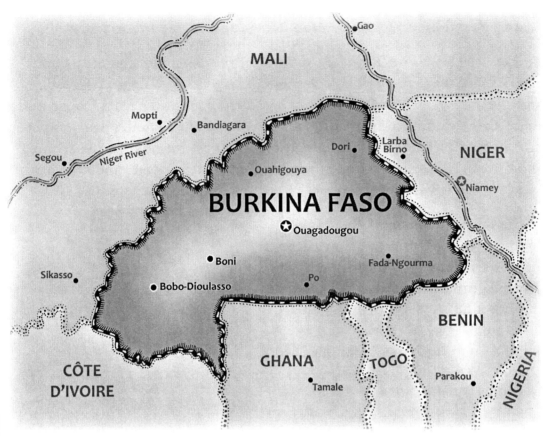

STANDARDS:
NA-M.K-4.8, 9
NA-M.5-8.8, 9
NSS-G.K-12.1, 2, 3, 4, 5
NL-ENG.K-12.3, 9

VITAL STATISTICS

Official Name:
Burkina Faso

Capital:
Ouagadougou

Area:
105,792 mi²

Population:
15.7 million

Currency:
CFA franc

Official Language:
French

Ethnic Groups:
Mossi, Jula, Bobo, Bwa, Fulani, Lobi, Gourma

Fact Sheet
BURKINA FASO

Burkina Faso is a **landlocked** country in the center of West Africa. Though it doesn't have a seaport, three rivers flow across Burkina: the Black Volta, the White Volta, and the Red Volta.

Historically, the area that is now Burkina Faso was dominated by two different forces: the *Mossi* Kingdom and the *Mande* Empire. As a result, Burkina shares many of the same musical instruments and **traditions** as countries like Mali and Guinea, which were also part of the Mande Empire, but also has some very *unique*

Learn to speak Mòoré
(a language from Burkina Faso)

MÒORÉ	ENGLISH
Ne i beogo. *(nay ee bay-oh-go)*	Good morning.
Beogo kibare? *(bay-oh-go key-ba-ray)*	How are you?
Laafi bala. *(lah-fee bah-lah)*	I am fine.
Barka! *(bar-kah)*	Thank you!
Nindaare. *(neen-dah-ray)*	Goodbye.

Burkina Faso
(bur-key-nah fah-so)

Burkinabé
(bur-key-nah-bay)
is the word used to refer to someone from Burkina Faso.

The **Mossi** people speak **Mòoré**.
(mou-ray)

Flag of Burkina Faso

FAMOUS MUSICIANS FROM BURKINA:
Farafina
Les Frères Coulibaly
Djiguiya

Ouagadougou
(wah-gah-dou-gou)

Did you know
that the name Burkina Faso means "Country of the People with **Integrity**" in the *Mòoré* and Jula languages? In 1984, Burkina's fourth president, Thomas Sankara, gave the country its new name, changing it from "Republic of Upper Volta."

During **Sankara's** presidency, he led the country to plant 1,000,000 mango trees. This effort to grow nutritious food, provide shade trees, and reduce **desertification** was a great success that Burkinabés still benefit from today.

traditions of its own. Today, Burkina Faso is a peaceful and friendly country shared by over 60 *ethnic groups*.

NORTHERN BURKINA

This area borders the countries of Mali and Niger, and it shares the dry climate of the *Sahel* with them. Northern Burkina is inhabited by many different peoples - *Fulani* and *Mossi*, among others. Most make their living from farming crops like *millet*, corn, and sesame.

KEY WORDS

BURKINA

landlocked .....
traditions .....
climate .....
integrity .....
sugar cane .....
desertification .....
mosque .....

CENTRAL BURKINA

This area shares parts of the dry, Sahelian climate of the north and the wet, *Sudanese* climate of the south. Central Burkina is dominated by the capital city, *Ouagadougou*, which is inhabited mostly by the Mossi people who make up over 40% of the country's population. Other ethnic groups that share this area are the *Jula, Bwa* and *Bobo*.

SOUTHERN BURKINA

Most of Burkina's south is in the green Sudanese zone. In contrast to the dry Sahel areas of the north, this area receives much more rainfall, and people grow **sugar cane** and cotton for a living. Southern Burkina borders the countries of Côte d'Ivoire and Ghana, and it's inhabited primarily by the *Lobi* people.

The famous mud **mosque** of Bobo-Dioulasso

STANDARDS:
NA-M.K-4.8, 9
NA-M.5-8.8, 9
NA-D.K-4.5
NA-D.5-8.5
NL-ENG.K-12.3, 9

BURKINA FASO

Journal Entry #12: Ouagadougou
THE LANGUAGE OF DANCE

The dancer, Aisha

From Niger, we buy a couple of seats on a **bush taxi** to take us over the border to our next destination, Burkina Faso. We're packed into a 12-seat passenger van with 24 people and several chickens. A tower of baggage, nets filled with onions, and 5 or 6 live sheep are tied to the top of the taxi. It's a miracle the van doesn't tip over from all the weight!

Somehow, we manage to reach the border, and we're greeted by some of the friendliest border officers we've ever met. They beam happiness at our arrival, and smile their greeting, "*Bienvenue au Burkina Faso!*" as they stamp our *passports*. This warm greeting is a reminder of Burkina's friendly reputation. The name Burkina Faso translates to "Country of the People with *Integrity*." We notice the effort that people make to welcome visitors and create an enjoyable environment for everyone.

After our border crossing, we have a few hours more to go until we reach our final stop for the day, Burkina Faso's capital city, *Ouagadougou*. There, we plan to meet up with a friend, *Aisha*, who dances in a local drum and dance performance group. They are practicing for a show at this year's FESPACO celebration. FESPACO is an **international** film festival that happens in Ouagadougou every two years, and the entire city gets swept up in preparations for the event.

We arrive in Ouagadougou and head directly to the stage where Aisha's group is practicing. She waves to us, and we take a seat to watch

Ouagadougou
(*Wah-gah-dou-gou*)

A **bush taxi** is a type of passenger vehicle common in West Africa. They often cross long distances between cities, where there's little to see except trees, sand, and bushes – hence the title "bush" taxi. Each person pays for a seat, and when the taxi is full, it will depart. Usually, bush taxis are over-loaded with people and goods.

"Bienvenue" = "Welcome" in French

Aisha
(*Ah-yee-sha*)

FESPACO is Africa's largest and most important film festival, attended by filmmakers and movie buffs from all over Africa and the world.

gita *(gee-tah)*

the **rehearsal** which is already underway. On stage is a troupe of 2 dancers and 4 *percussionists*. The percussionists play *balafons, djembes, dunduns,* and a type of shaker made from a *calabash* and *cowrie shells,* called a **gita**. Moving to the rhythm, the dancers express activities of daily life in Burkina Faso – planting seeds, *harvesting* crops, pounding grain, making a fire, cooking, carrying water, caring for children, celebrating, competing, and even a **masquerade** dance.

After the rehearsal, we ask Aisha to explain their dance performance. She says, "Through our dance, we want to tell a story of what it means to live in a *traditional* village in Burkina Faso. Many foreigners will come to Ouagadougou for FESPACO, without an opportunity to see what life is like outside of the city. We want to show the world that our traditional **culture** is alive and beautiful. The language of the dance allows us to express these things without words."

Comprehension Questions:

1) Describe the taxi that the travelers take from Niger to Burkina Faso.

2) How does the name Burkina Faso translate to English?

3) What is FESPACO?

4) Which percussion instruments are part of Aisha's performance group?

5) What do the dancers express in their performance?

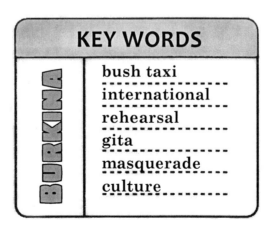

KEY WORDS	
BURKINA	bush taxi
	international
	rehearsal
	gita
	masquerade
	culture

Art Connection: **Bwa Hawk Mask** *(pg. 216)*

STANDARDS:
NA-M.K-4.8, 9
NA-M.5-8.8, 9
NA-VA.K-4.4, 6
NA-VA.5-8.4, 5, 6
NA-D.K-4.5
NA-D.5-8.3
NSS-G.K-12.2
NL-ENG.K-12.3, 9

Bwa Butterfly Mask

BURKINA FASO

Journal Entry #13: Boni

THE BWA: MASTERS OF THE MASQUERADE

Bobo-Dioulasso
(boh-boh dee-ou-lah-so)

Boni *(bow-knee)*

Today we're traveling with our dancer friend, Aisha. We're heading west, from Ouagadougou to Burkina Faso's second largest city and cultural capital, *Bobo-Dioulasso*.

On the road to Bobo, we stop for lunch in a village called *Boni*. It's market day, and the town is bustling with activity. *Merchants* are selling things like fruit, rice, spices, and colorful fabrics. It's a festive atmosphere, and people are smiling and talking all around us.

Suddenly, we hear the sound of a drum in the distance. Aisha exclaims, "Masks! Look..." and she points to the edge of the market where a tall spike painted black, red, and white dances in the air to the beat of the drum. "That is the Bwa serpent mask. Each village tries to make the biggest, most impressive serpent mask. This one looks really big!" We see that the mask must be at least 15 feet tall. Even though we can't see the dancer who wears the mask, we know that he must be a very strong man to wear such a large and heavy wooden mask.

After the serpent mask, an amazing variety of other animal masks join the dance – antelopes, **hyenas**, buffalos, monkeys, **bush pigs**, crocodiles, fish, hawks, and even butterflies. Each of these masks dances in a way that **mimics** the behavior of the animal. The antelope bucks, prances, and stamps his feet, making a great show of his beautiful horns. The butterfly, covered in an impressive pattern of eight targets, twirls left and right, then comes to rest as if perched on a flower before flying away again. The bush pig paws at the ground with his feet, throwing up clouds of dust, and sniffing the air for the scent of danger.

Each of the masks is carved from wood and painted with three colors: red, black, and white. The **geometric** designs are very striking, with patterns of lines, squares, zigzags, and **crescents** that *symbolize* important concepts to the Bwa people. Costumes of long, black and red fibers are attached to the wooden masks, and they swirl around as the dancers move.

The *masquerade* is **accompanied** by an *ensemble* of musicians unlike anything we've ever heard. The strangest sound is made by a **chorus** of high-pitched whistles, which create an *eerie* song on top of the *melodies* played on *balafons*. This music is accompanied by drummers, who play two types of drums: a long, skinny drum like a big *kalangou* and a round bass drum like the *doundoun* that we saw in Niger. It is fascinating to watch the interaction between the masked dancers and the music. Every mask has a different dance and song.

The Bwa are an *ethnic group* that live in Burkina Faso and Mali. They are famous for their beautiful masks.

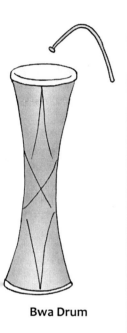

Bwa Drum

Comprehension Questions:

1) What kinds of things are being sold at the market in Boni?

2) About how tall is the serpent mask?

3) What types of animal masks do the travelers see?

4) How do the different masks dance?

4) What musical instruments accompany the mask dance in Boni?

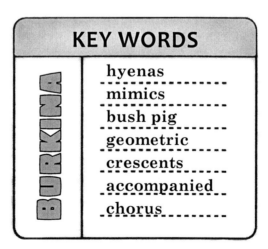

KEY WORDS

BURKINA

hyenas
mimics
bush pig
geometric
crescents
accompanied
chorus

STANDARDS:
NA-M.K-4.8, 9
NA-M.5-8.8, 9
NL-ENG.K-12.3, 9

BURKINA FASO

Journal Entry #14: Bobo-Dioulasso
BURKINA'S MUSICAL HEARTLAND

Bobo-Dioulasso
(boh-boh dee-ou-lah-so)

drumming and dancing at Les Bambous

Today's adventure takes us to the musical heart and soul of Burkina Faso: *Bobo-Dioulasso*. This city is remarkable for its rich *tradition* of drum and dance *ensembles*. Performance groups sprout up all over the city and compete with each other to be the best. This tradition has a long history in Bobo, and as a result, the drum and dance groups have developed a very high level of skill and talent. Some of the most successful ensembles from Bobo have gone on to tour the world and perform at the best concert halls in the world.

Bobo-Dioulasso is sometimes referred to as simply "Bobo." Burkina Faso's second largest city, Bobo-Dioulasso is named after the Bobo and Jula (or Dioula) people who have lived there for many years.

We have come to Bobo to get a taste of this *unique* local tradition, and with our friend Aisha as our guide, we're sure to experience something special. She knows exactly where to take us first: to *Les Bambous*. This is a club where the Bobo drum and dance groups come to perform. Over the years, thousands of local groups have **debuted** their shows on the Les Bambous stage.

"Les Bambous" is French for "The Bamboos."

Aisha explains the seriousness of Bobo's performing groups, "Many times, the performances are developed and practiced in complete secrecy so that none of the other groups can steal their ideas. Every time a group performs, they are aiming to be the best. Even more, they hope for an opportunity to make it big with a world tour, a record deal, or another **breakthrough** like that."

We sit down for dinner, and the show starts. A young man walks onto the stage with a *djembe* strapped around his shoulders. He plays a signal on his drum, and all of the djembe, *dundun*, and *balafon* players play an exciting **drum break** in **unison** to begin the show. They play with a force that vibrates the lights overhead. Three dancers emerge from the side of the stage, and the performance quickly heats up into a blaze of sound and action.

Makossa
(mah-koh-sa)

Aisha says, "This song is the *Makossa*. It's about a girl from the village who is a great dancer. Her name is Aisha, too! Come on, let's dance!"

She pulls us to the dance floor and we join the growing crowd dancing to the Makossa beat. The performance group smiles and looks satisfied as they continue to play. The participation of the audience is proof that they have succeeded tonight, even without a major breakthrough. The music is irresistible!

Later, we have a chance to meet the drummers, and they teach us how to play the Makossa song and rhythm. It's a fantastic end to a fabulous rhythm hunting adventure through West Africa!

Comprehension Questions:

1) What do the travelers say is remarkable about Bobo-Dioulasso?

2) How have the performing groups evolved to a very high level of accomplishment in Bobo?

3) What are many of the groups aiming to accomplish?

4) What instruments are played by the performing group?

5) What shows the ensemble that they have been successful tonight?

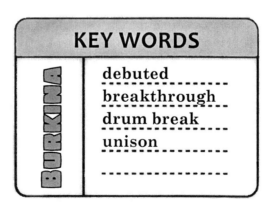

jamming on djembes in Burkina Faso

THE MUSIC

ABOUT THE MUSIC

DRUM RHYTHMS & XYLOPHONE OSTINATI

In *Drumming Up World Music: West Africa,* we refer to an individual drum part as a "rhythm." **Low Drum (LD), High Drum (HD)** and **Percussion (PR)** all play rhythms. An individual xylophone part is referred to as an "ostinato" (plural, "ostinati"). In the xylophone arrangements, ostinati are played by **Bass (BX), Alto (AX)**, and **Soprano (SX)** xylophones in Levels 1-5. In Levels 4 and 5, the Soprano Xylophone also plays **Melody 1 (M1)** and **Melody 2 (M2)**, in addition to its ostinato pattern.

DVD & CD

The DVD and CD have video and audio demonstrations of the arrangements in this book. Select music notations are included as images on the DVD, so teachers can present them to students using a video projector.

SIGNATURE RHYTHM & OSTINATO

Each drum and xylophone arrangement has a Signature Rhythm or Ostinato. This pattern is called "Signature" because it's the main part of the music, and it defines the character of each arrangement. The Signature part is played by the Bass Xylophone (BX) and the Low Drum (LD). We recommend teaching the Signature part for each arrangement when you first introduce a song to your students. Learning how to play the Signature pattern builds a strong foundation for the rest of the song and offers a first glimpse into the music from each country featured in the book.

DRUM BREAKS & BREAK ENDINGS

In the drum arrangements, there are "Drum Breaks" that are played in unison by all drums and percussion at the beginning and end of the piece. In the xylophone arrangements, there are "Break Endings" that are played in unison by all of the xylophones, drums, and percussion at end of the piece. Both of these are optional additions to the drum and xylophone arrangements.

LEARNING LEVELS

This book features arrangements in 4/4, 4/4 swing, 3/4, and 6/8 time. Rather than rating each of these arrangements as beginning, intermediate, or advanced, we have developed what we call "Learning Levels" for each arrangement. Learning Levels give teachers the flexibility to raise or lower the difficulty level of the music to match the skill level of each class.

LEARNING LEVELS FOR DRUM ARRANGEMENTS

NOTATION KEY
LD = Low Drum
HD = High Drum
PR = Percussion
DB = Drum Break

LEVEL 1 — **Introduce Signature Rhythm (LD)**
LD, HD & PR play Signature Rhythm

LEVEL 2 — **Introduce HD Rhythm**
LD & PR play Signature Rhythm
HD plays HD Rhythm

LEVEL 3 — **Introduce PR Rhythm**
LD plays Signature Rhythm
HD plays HD Rhythm - PR plays PR Rhythm

LEVEL 4 — **Play Full Arrangement with Drum Break (DB)**
DB + Level 3 + DB

BREAK — **DRUM BREAK** — **OPTIONAL: Drum Break**
All instruments play DB in unison
DB can be played at any level

LEARNING LEVELS FOR XYLOPHONE ARRANGEMENTS

NOTATION KEY
SX = Soprano Xylo.
AX = Alto Xylophone
BX = Bass Xylophone
LD = Low Drum
PR = Percussion
M1 = Melody 1
M2 = Melody 2

LEVEL 1 — **Introduce Signature Bass Ostinato (BX)**
BX, AX, SX play Signature Ostinato

LEVEL 2 — **Introduce Alto Ostinato (AX)**
BX & SX play Signature Ostinato
AX plays AX Ostinato

LEVEL 3 — **Introduce Soprano Ostinato (SX)**
BX plays Signature Ostinato
AX plays AX Ostinato, SX plays SX Ostinato

LEVEL 4 — **Melody 1 (M1) Arrangement**
Level 3 + M1 + downbeat ending

LEVEL 5 — **Full Arrangement**
Level 3 + M1 + M2 + M2 Ending

BREAK — **BREAK ENDING** — **OPTIONAL: Introduce Break Ending (BE)**
All instruments play BE in unison
BE can be played at any level

LAYERING

All of the arrangements in this book are presented using the concept of layering, as the parts of the music are added one on top of the other in sequence throughout the piece. This helps students hear how the rhythms and ostinati fit together in time. Here is an example of how we use layering in this book:

Drum Layering

1. Low Drum (LD) plays as 1st layer
2. High Drum (HD) joins LD as 2nd layer
3. Percussion (PR) joins LD and HD as 3rd Layer

Xylophone Layering

1. Bass Xylophone (BX) and Percussion (PR) play as 1st layer
2. Alto Xylophone (AX) plays and joins BX and PR as 2nd layer
3. Soprano Xylophone (SX) plays and joins BX, PR, and AX as 3rd layer
4. Low Drum (LD) plays and joins BX, PR, AX, and SX as 4th layer

This method of layering works for both unison and polyrhythmic playing. You can switch the order of layering, layer in or layer out, or choose to not use layering and have all of the instruments start at the same time.

TEMPO

We have included recommended tempos for each drum and xylophone arrangement that present the music at a moderate speed for teaching. You can set the tempo faster or slower to best suit your preference, the skill level of your class, or for student performances.

XYLOPHONE ARRANGEMENT WITH DRUM & PERCUSSION ACCOMPANIMENT

All of the xylophone arrangements are presented with drum and percussion accompaniment. The drum accompaniment is the Signature Rhythm played by the Low Drum (LD). The percussion accompaniment plays the pulse of the music at the very beginning of the piece along with the Bass Xylophone to help mark the time. Both of these drum and percussion accompaniment parts are optional and do not need to be played in the arrangement. We did not include the High Drum (HD) and Percussion (PR) rhythms from the drum arrangements as part of this accompaniment, but you can use them if you would like to add more rhythmic accompaniment to the xylophone arrangements.

Melody Arrangements for Xylophones - Levels 4 & 5

After learning and playing the xylophone ostinati in Levels 1, 2, and 3, your students will be ready to add Melody 1 (M1) and Melody 2 (M2). These melodies are introduced and played in Levels 4 and 5 on the Soprano Xylophone (SX). In Level 4, students will learn and play Melody 1. In Level 5, students will learn and play Melody 2 and the Melody 2 ending. Both Level 4 and 5 have two sections of instruction. The first section introduces the melody by itself. The second section of Level 4 shows how Melody 1 fits with the parts played by the Bass and Alto Xylophones. The second section of Level 5 features the Full Arrangement, beginning with the Level 3 ostinati and adding Melodies 1 and 2.

Teaching Tools

Rhythm Phonics

Numerous world drumming traditions throughout history have used the spoken word to communicate rhythmic phrases. Musicians in Africa, India, the Middle East, and the Caribbean, for example, use words to mimic sounds on the drums, and phrases of "drum talk" to communicate rhythms. Sheet music and standard notation are relatively new developments in the long history of drumming.

In this book, we rely heavily on the oral traditions of teaching rhythms by vocalizing them through a system that we call "Rhythm Phonics." Based on the concept of "if you can say it, you can play it," Rhythm Phonics can be used to teach drum rhythms and xylophone ostinati.

To teach the drum rhythms with Rhythm Phonics, we use two verbal methods: **Words & Syllables**, which connect the beats of a rhythm with the syllables of a phrase, creating a song for the rhythm, and **Drum Sounds**, using the word "Boom" for the low sound of the drum and "Ba" for the high sound.

In addition to the Rhythm Phonics charts, we've included Standard Notation for each arrangement. The Rhythm Phonics and Standard Notation are two different representations of the same music.

To teach the xylophone ostinati in this book, we have created simple

In Dancing Drum's **Rhythm Phonics** system of notation, "O" stands for the "Boom" sound and "X" stands for the "Ba" sound.

KEY	LOW	MID/HI
SOUND	Boom	Ba
SYMBOL	O	X

In **Standard Notation,** a high note on the staff stands for "Ba", and a low note on the staff stands for "Boom".

phrases with words and syllables following the rhythm of the xylophone notes. These phrases are meant to be used as teaching tools for students to connect the rhythm of what they say to the rhythm of what they play. The phrases do not have any meaning in relationship to the songs, other than to be used as a teaching tool.

Call-and-Response

Call-and-Response is one of the most simple and useful tools for leading rhythms, and it's an essential part of teaching with Rhythm Phonics. The principle is simple: the leader creates a "Call" by speaking the rhythmic phrase with Rhythm Phonics or by playing a percussion instrument. As soon as the call ends, the class echoes the pattern together in "Response". The leader can play a sequence of different rhythms with variations in tempo and complexity to challenge the group.

Lap-Clap Body Percussion

Lap = "Boom"

Lap-Clap Body Percussion is a kinesthetic sensory motor system for learning rhythms. Students strike their laps with their hands to make the "Boom" sound and clap their hands to make the "Ba" sound. Lap-Clap Body Percussion is an excellent way to connect motor skills with the rhythm before moving on to the drums.

Ready Position

Ready Position means that students are in position to play, hands and sticks pausing just above the playing surface of the drums or xylophones. They are quiet and listening, waiting for instructions. Demonstrate "Ready Position" on each instrument and have your class practice showing that they are ready to play.

Clap = "Ba"

Classroom Set-Up

Create instrument sections by grouping the same types of drums, percussion, and xylophones together to make a semi-circular "percussion orchestra." Place the low drums with the low drums and the high drums with the high drums. The different pitches of xylophones should sit next to each other, so that students in each section can support each other in the part that they play.

It's ideal if each section has an equal number of instruments so that you can set up your class in rotation groups that move through each section in turn. This way, every student gets a chance to play each type of instrument.

SOLOING & IMPROVISATION ON DRUM ARRANGEMENTS

Soloing and improvisation allow for individual drummers to have the spotlight for a moment and develop their own unique "voice" or style that they can play in addition to the arranged rhythms and breaks.

Teachers can provide opportunities for student soloing with any of the drum arrangements in this book. To highlight a student who would like to take a solo, the teacher can direct an instrument section or two drop out for a few measures while the soloist plays. This will allow the soloist to be better heard by the audience and the rest of the ensemble. For example, the teacher may instruct all of the djembes to stop, while the djun-djuns and percussionists continue to play. The djembe soloist then improvises over the djun-djuns and percussion while the rest of the djembes listen, or clap the pulse of the rhythm supportively. Soloists can also play over the sound of the entire ensemble, however it works best if the group brings the volume down to a level where the soloist can be heard. Make sure that your class understands that solo means "alone" or "on one's own" and the solo should be played by only one person at a time.

Here are a few concepts to present to your students when adding a solo to the drum arrangements:

a) Play a simple solo phrase that's one or two measures long.
b) Repeat the phrase at least twice.
c) Continue with another short rhythmic phrase (one or two measures), and repeat it at least twice again.
d) As you progress, make the solo phrases longer than 2 measures.
e) Drummers can diversify their soloing by playing different drum sounds in the same pattern, or adding or removing notes to give the phrase a new feel.

NATIONAL STANDARDS

The National Standards for Arts Education that are covered by the music in this book include:

NA-M.l-4.1, 2, 3, 5, 6, 8, & 9
NA-M.5-8.1, 2, 3, 5, 6, 8, & 9

For more information on these standards, please visit the "Curriculum Connections" chapter that begins on page 14.

FUNDAMENTALS OF DRUMMING

This section briefly covers some of the important aspects of drumming as it is utilized in *Drumming Up World Music: West Africa*. After reading, make sure to spend some time watching and playing along with the DVD. The DVD demonstrates the drumming fundamentals and covers each arrangement in this book. It's designed to be a comprehensive resource that teachers can use to prepare for class, and the DVD, along with the CD, can be used to help introduce new material to students.

INSTRUMENTATION

Drumming Up World Music: West Africa has a recommended instrumentation, however we've set it up to be as flexible as possible. In Dancing Drum's school programs, we utilize a large number of instruments to actively engage every student in playing the music. This is the ideal situation, however we understand that not every music teacher will have the resources to provide each student with a drum or xylophone. Our hope is that, through creating a system that uses a flexible set-up, more teachers will be able to access the learning materials in this program.

The **Low Drum** (LD), **High Drum** (HD), and **Percussion** (PR) designations are kept purposefully vague so that music teachers will feel free to adapt the instrumentation. Below is a list of options that would work for each part, with recommended instruments in **bold**:

Low Drum (LD) - Any low-tuned drums, including **djun-djuns** (dunduns), tubanos, congas, bass drums, and djembes

High Drum (HD) - Any high-tuned drums, including **djembes**, tubanos, congas, bongos, and dumbeks

Percussion (PR) - Depending on the arrangement, shakers (**shekeres**, maracas, axatse, caxixi), bells (**cowbell**, agogo, gankogui), blocks (**woodblocks**, claves, rhythm sticks), scrapers (**kariyan**, guiros)

If your classroom only has a few drums, tune the drums that you have to make a low drum section and a high drum section, and fill in the rest with percussion.

djun-djuns *(june-junes)* are also called dunduns, dununs, & doons

RECOMMENDED DRUMS

djembe (jem-bay)

tilting the djembe

Agogo
double bell

Since all drumming parts in this book are set up using 2 tones (low and high) teachers can use a double bell to introduce or reinforce drumming parts.

Djembe

The *djembe* is a type of hand drum from the West African countries of Mali, Guinea, Burkina Faso, Côte D'Ivoire, Sierra Leone, Liberia, and Senegal. Historically, these countries were part of the ancient Mande Empire. This region is where the djembe was created hundreds of years ago, and there are many different stories about exactly how the first djembe was made. According to the Bamana people of Mali, the name djembe comes from the saying *"Anke dje, anke be"* which translates to "everyone gather together." Today, this powerful drum is played for all kinds of celebrations and events that bring people together in West Africa and throughout the world.

The shell of the djembe is shaped like a goblet and made of wood. The drumhead is traditionally made from a goatskin that is attached to the shell with metal rings and rope. Djembes are tuned by adding or removing what are called "diamonds" from the rope weave, which tightens or loosens the drumhead for a higher or lower sound.

For this program, we'll focus on making two clear sounds on the djembe: a low sound that we call **"Boom"** and a high sound that we call **"Ba"**. First, make sure that you're playing the drum correctly. Sit in a chair with the drum placed in front of you, between your knees. The top of the djembe should be slightly lower than your elbows. Tilt the drum and hold it at an angle so that the bottom is open, allowing the full range of sounds to be made on the drum. Don't let the bottom of the drum rest flat on the floor because this will trap the sound inside. Beginners who have difficulty holding the drum properly may want to use a drum stand.

Practice playing the "Boom" sound

Place the palm of your hand flat in the middle of the drumhead. Raise your hand and let it fall. Your hand should bounce off the drum so that the maximum bass sound resonates from the skin. Practice the "Boom" sound by alternating your right and left hands in the middle of your drum, playing a steady drum roll.

The "Boom" sound is in the middle

Practice playing the "Ba" sound

Place your hand on the edge of the drum closest to you. Your hand should fit on the rim of the drum along your knuckles. The rest of your hand, including your thumb, will hang off the side. There should be a point where your hands find a comfortable spot along the rim of the drum. Now raise your hand and give the drum a light tap. This motion makes a high-pitched tone called "Ba." Your hand should bounce up with each strike. Now practice the Ba sound by playing a slow and steady drum roll.

The "Ba" sound is on the edge

Djun-Djuns

Djun-Djuns are West African bass drums played alongside the djembe. They are also known as *dunduns, dununs,* or *doons*. Played with sticks, the djun-djuns make a powerful, low-pitched sound that compliments the higher sound of the djembe.

The shell of a djun-djun is made from wood and shaped like a cylinder. Djuns have two skins – one on top and one on the bottom. The drumheads are traditionally made from cow hide, and they are attached to the drum shell with metal rings and rope. Tuning the drum is accomplished by tightening or loosening the ropes to make the pitch higher or lower.

3 Djun-Djuns on stands
kenkeni, dundunba, & sangban (L-R)

Djun-djuns come in three different sizes. The largest drum is called "*dundunba*", the middle-sized drum is named "*sangban*", and the smallest djun-djun is called "*kenkeni*".

Djun-djuns can be played in many different ways – in sets of one, two, three, or more drums. Djun-djun drummers usually stand while playing. For the Dru*mming Up World Music* program, we usually play with one djun-djun per student, with the drums set up on stands. If you prefer, this program can be easily adapted to play with two djuns per student, with one high drum and one low drum each.

A Note about Traditional Djembe Technique:

Traditional djembe technique utilizes three distinct sounds called *Bass, Tone,* and *Slap*. Bass and tone are basically the same as the "Boom" and "Ba" sounds that we use in Dancing Drum's elementary and middle school programs. The slap sound is higher pitched than the Ba sound, and it takes dedicated practice and time to achieve.

A Note about Traditional Djun-Djun Technique:

In West Africa, drummers play djun-djuns in several different ways. "Traditional" or "Guinea" style uses one djun-djun placed sideways on a stand with a bell. A more modern style of playing, known as "Ballet" style, places the djun-djuns upright for playing in a set of two, three, or more.

The following instructions will help you start playing the djun-djuns:

Practice playing the "Boom" sound

Place your sticks in the middle of your djun-djun and strike it so that the sticks bounce off the drum head. This will make the "Boom" sound. You can hit the drum with both sticks at once ("Sticks Together"), or you can play with one stick at a time, alternating right and left ("Hand-Over-Hand").

Practice playing the "Ba" sound

For the "Ba" sound, move your sticks to the outside edge of the drum and strike the rim. Your sticks should hang over the edge by an inch or two, so that your hit creates a wooden "clack" sound. There should be no sound of the drum head with this technique, only wood.

Split Sticking

Many of the arrangements in this book work best with "Split Sticking", with one stick playing the "Boom" sound and the other stick playing the "Ba" sound throughout the rhythm.

The "Boom" sound is in the middle

The "Ba" sound is on the edge

"Split Sticking" dedicates one stick to "Boom" and the other to "Ba"

Percussion

Drumming Up World Music: West Africa incorporates a variety of shakers, scrapers, bells, and blocks. The arrangements in this volume include one small percussion part each. The DVD that comes with this book shows how to play each part on the different percussion instruments. You can use the percussion instruments that we recommend, or use whatever you have available in your classroom.

shekere

Reading Connection: **Journal #2 - Dakar** *(pg. 32)*

N'DAAGA

N'Daaga is a rhythm from Senegal. It's mainly played by the *Wolof* people in Senegal's capital city, Dakar.

This is one of the first rhythms that many Senegalese children learn to dance to, and it's the first rhythm that our travelers encounter in West Africa.

N'Daaga is usually played on *sabar* drums. Sabar drummers play a high pitched sound with a thin stick in one hand, and make a lower pitched sound with the palm of the other hand.

N'Daaga is a versatile, 3/4 rhythm that can be used to *accompany* other songs. In the Senegal xylophone section, this rhythm accompanies the song *Miyaabele*.

Sabar master, Bara M'Boup, playing sabar with hand & stick

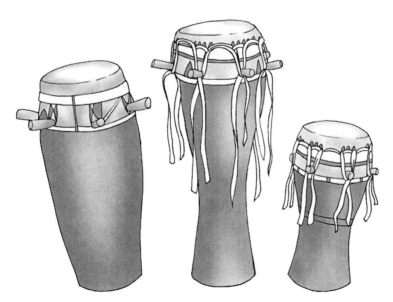

Wolof Sabar Drums: Chol, Nder, Toumouni

N'Daaga Highlights:

N'Daaga is played in 3/4 time with a "waltz" feel. It showcases the sabar style of drumming from Senegal, with a powerful drum break and galloping rhythm. When played to accompany the Miyaabele Xylophone song, the 4th bar of the N'Daaga Signature Rhythm has an 8th note pattern that signals a chord change.

SENEGAL

♩ = 130 *Recommended Tempo*

N'DAAGA
DRUM

SUGGESTED ARRANGEMENT

Levels 1-3

Level 1 = 1 part polyrhythm
Level 2 = 2 part polyrhythm
Level 3 = 3 part polyrhythm
Level 4 = 3 part polyrhythm
+ drum break

1. LD plays 8 bars , then HD plays.
2. LD and HD play 8 bars, then PR plays.
3. LD, HD , and PR play for 16 bars or as long as desired.
4. Play downbeat ending.
5. Go back to measure 1 and repeat for longer arrangement.

Level 4

1. Add Drum Break (DB) to beginning and end of Level 3 arrangement. All instruments play Drum Break in unison.
2. Play DB at beginning, count 3 quarter notes, and begin Level 3 arrangement. To end Level 3 arrangement, play downbeat ending, count 3 quarter notes, and finish with the final DB.

*** Drum Break for Levels 1 & 2 (Optional)** - Drum Break can also be played at the beginning and end of Level 1-2 arrangements. Level 4 = Level 3 + Drum Break.*

LEARNING LEVELS

LEVEL 1	★☆☆☆	**Introduce Signature Rhythm (LD)** LD, HD & PR play Signature Rhythm
LEVEL 2	★★☆☆	**Introduce HD Rhythm** LD & PR play Signature Rhythm HD plays HD Rhythm
LEVEL 3	★★★☆	**Introduce PR Rhythm** LD plays Signature Rhythm HD plays HD Rhythm - PR plays PR Rhythm
LEVEL 4	★★★★	**Play Full Arrangement with Drum Break (DB)** DB + Level 3 + DB
BREAK	**DRUM BREAK**	**OPTIONAL: Drum Break** DB can be played at any level All instruments play DB in unison

SENEGAL

Introduce Signature Rhythm
LD, HD & PR play Signature Rhythm

CD Track: 1

NOTATION KEY
LD = Low Drum
HD = High Drum
PR = Percussion

KEY	LOW	MID/HIGH
SOUND	Boom	Ba
SYMBOL	O	X

N'DAAGA
DRUM

Signature Rhythm (LD) - Rhythm Phonics   Traditional, arranged by Dancing Drum

LD

3/4	1	&	2	&	3	&	1	&	2	&	3	&
W/S	N'		Daa		ga		N'		Daa		ga	
O/X	O		X		X		O		X		X	

3/4	1	&	2	&	3	&	1	&	2	&	3	&
W/S	N'		Daa		ga		Let's	all		play	the	
O/X	O		X		X		O	O		O	O	

W/S = Words & Syllables; **O/X** = Boom & Ba

HD

3/4	1	&	2	&	3	&	1	&	2	&	3	&
W/S	N'		Daa		ga		N'		Daa		ga	
O/X	O		X		X		O		X		X	

3/4	1	&	2	&	3	&	1	&	2	&	3	&
W/S	N'		Daa		ga		Let's	all		play	the	
O/X	O		X		X		O	O		O	O	

PR

3/4	1	&	2	&	3	&	1	&	2	&	3	&
W/S	N'		Daa		ga		N'		Daa		ga	
O/X	X		X		X		X		X		X	

3/4	1	&	2	&	3	&	1	&	2	&	3	&
W/S	N'		Daa		ga		Let's	all		play	the	
O/X	X		X		X		X	X		X	X	

Dancing Drum © 2010

Introduce Signature Rhythm
LD, HD, & PR play Signature Rhythm

N'DAAGA
DRUM

♩ = 130

Signature Rhythm (LD) - Standard Notation

Traditional, arranged by Dancing Drum

LD

LEVEL 2 ★★☆☆

CD Track: 2

Introduce HD Rhythm
LD & PR play Signature Rhythm
HD plays HD Rhythm

KEY	LOW	MID/HIGH
SOUND	Boom	Ba
SYMBOL	O	X

N'DAAGA
DRUM

HD Rhythm - Rhythm Phonics
Traditional, arranged by Dancing Drum

HD

3/4	1	&	2	&	3	&	1	&	2	&	3	&
W/S	Se	ne	gal		drum		Se	ne	gal		drum	
O/X	X	X	X		O		X	X	X		O	

W/S = Words & Syllables; O/X = Boom & Ba

LD

3/4	1	&	2	&	3	&	1	&	2	&	3	&
W/S	N'		Daa		ga		N'		Daa		ga	
O/X	O		X		X		O		X		X	

3/4	1	&	2	&	3	&	1	&	2	&	3	&
W/S	N'		Daa		ga		Let's	all		play	the	
O/X	O		X		X		O	O		O	O	

HD

3/4	1	&	2	&	3	&	1	&	2	&	3	&
W/S	Se	ne	gal		drum		Se	ne	gal		drum	
O/X	X	X	X		O		X	X	X		O	

PR

3/4	1	&	2	&	3	&	1	&	2	&	3	&
W/S	N'		Daa		ga		N'		Daa		ga	
O/X	X		X		X		X		X		X	

3/4	1	&	2	&	3	&	1	&	2	&	3	&
W/S	N'		Daa		ga		Let's	all		play	the	
O/X	X		X		X		X	X		X	X	

Dancing Drum © 2010

CD Track: **2**

N'DAAGA

DRUM

♩ = 130

HD Rhythm - Standard Notation

Traditional, arranged by Dancing Drum

Se - ne - gal drum Se - ne - gal drum

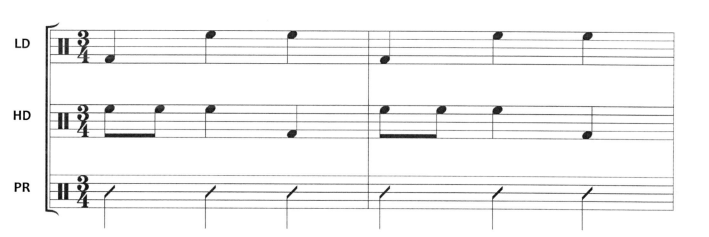

Dancing Drum © 2010

Introduce PR Rhythm
LD plays Signature Rhythm
HD plays HD Rhythm - PR plays PR Rhythm

KEY	LOW	MID/HIGH
SOUND	Boom	Ba
SYMBOL	O	X

N'DAAGA
DRUM

PR Rhythm - Rhythm Phonics

Traditional, arranged by Dancing Drum

PR

3/4	1	&	2	&	3	&	1	&	2	&	3	&
W/S	Play		N'	Daa	ga		from		Se	ne	gal	
O/X	X		X	X	X		X		X	X	X	

W/S = Words & Syllables; O/X = Boom & Ba

LD

3/4	1	&	2	&	3	&	1	&	2	&	3	&
W/S	N'		Daa		ga		N'		Daa		ga	
O/X	O		X		X		O		X		X	

3/4	1	&	2	&	3	&	1	&	2	&	3	&
W/S	N'		Daa		ga		Let's	all		play	the	
O/X	O		X		X		O	O		O	O	

HD

3/4	1	&	2	&	3	&	1	&	2	&	3	&
W/S	Se	ne	gal		drum		Se	ne	gal		drum	
O/X	X	X	X		O		X	X	X		O	

PR

3/4	1	&	2	&	3	&	1	&	2	&	3	&
W/S	Play		N'	Daa	ga		from		Se	ne	gal	
O/X	X		X	X	X		X		X	X	X	

Dancing Drum © 2010

Introduce PR Rhythm
LD plays Signature Rhythm
HD plays HD Rhythm - PR plays PR Rhythm

CD Track: **3**

N'DAAGA
DRUM

PR Rhythm - Standard Notation

Traditional, arranged by Dancing Drum

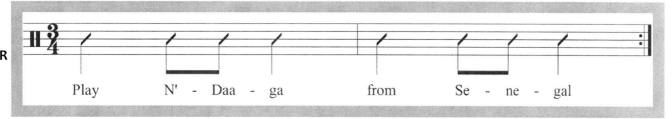

Play   N' - Daa - ga   from   Se - ne - gal

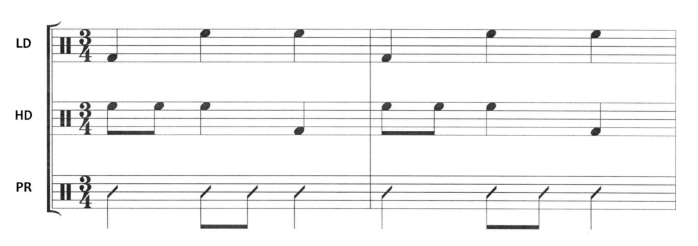

Dancing Drum © 2010

 **DRUM BREAK**

OPTIONAL: Drum Break
All instruments play DB in unison
DB can be played at any level

CD Track: **4**

NOTATION KEY
LD = Low Drum
HD = High Drum
PR = Percussion
DB = Drum Break

KEY	LOW	MID/HIGH
SOUND	Boom	Ba
SYMBOL	O	X

N'DAAGA
DRUM

Drum Break (DB) - Rhythm Phonics

Traditional, arranged by Dancing Drum

DB

3/4	1	&	2	&	3	&	1	&	2	&	3	&
W/S	Play	the	N'	Daa	ga		sa	bar	drum	break	now	
O/X	X	X	X	O	X		O	O	O	O	X	

3/4	1	&	2	&	3	&	1	&	2	&	3	&
W/S	Play	it	on	your	drum		like		you	know	how	
O/X	X	X	X	O	X		O		O	O	O	

Drum Break (DB) - Standard Notation

DB

Play the N' - Daa - ga   sa - bar   drum   break   now

Play   it   on   your   drum   like   you   know   how

LEVEL 4 ★★★★

CD Track: 5

Play Full Arrangement
DB + Level 3 + DB

NOTATION KEY
LD = Low Drum
HD = High Drum
PR = Percussion
DB = Drum Break

N'DAAGA
DRUM

♩ = 130

Full Arrangement

Traditional, arranged by Dancing Drum

Dancing Drum © 2010

West Africa 93

MIYAABELE
XYLOPHONE

SENEGAL

LEARNING LEVELS

LEVEL 1	★☆☆☆☆	**Introduce Signature Bass Ostinato (BX)** BX, AX, SX play Signature Ostinato
LEVEL 2	★★☆☆☆	**Introduce Alto Ostinato (AX)** BX & SX play Signature Ostinato AX plays AX Ostinato
LEVEL 3	★★★☆☆	**Introduce Soprano Ostinato (SX)** BX plays Signature Ostinato AX plays AX Ostinato, SX plays SX Ostinato
LEVEL 4	★★★★☆	**Melody 1 (M1) Arrangement** Level 3 + M1 + downbeat ending
LEVEL 5	★★★★★	**Full Arrangement** Level 3 + M1 + M2 + M2 Ending
BREAK	**Break Ending**	**OPTIONAL: Introduce Break Ending (BE)** All instruments play BE in unison BE can be played at any level

pirogues on the river

Miyaabele Highlights:

Miyaabele is a Fulani folk song played in 3/4 time with a "waltz" feel. This song changes chords every 4 bars during the Level 1-3 ostinati and Melody 1. The N'Daaga rhythm that accompanies Miyaabele has an 8th note pattern in the 4th bar that signals this chord change. During Melody 2, the chord change switches to every 2 bars instead of every 4 bars. Here, the 8th note pattern of the N'Daaga rhythm accents the same 8th note pattern found in Melody 2. Miyaabele showcases the rhythms and melodies of Senegal as a beautiful African waltz.

NOTATION KEY
SX = Soprano Xylophone
AX = Alto Xylophone
BX = Bass Xylophone
LD = Low Drum
PR = Percussion
M1 = Melody 1
M2 = Melody 2

MIYAABELE

XYLOPHONE

SUGGESTED ARRANGEMENT

Level 1 = 1 part ostinato
Level 2 = 2 part ostinato
Level 3 = 3 part ostinato
Level 4 = 3 part ostinato + M1
Level 5 = 3 part ostinato + M1 + M2

Levels 1-3

1. BX, PR play 8 bars, then AX plays. (Chord changes every 4 bars.)

2. BX, PR and AX play 8 bars, then SX plays.

3. BX, PR, AX, and SX play for 8 bars, then LD plays.

4. All instruments play ostinati for 16 bars or as many as desired.

5. Play downbeat ending.

6. Go back to measure 1 and repeat for longer arrangement.

Level 4

1. BX, PR play 8 bars, then AX plays. (Chord changes every 4 bars.)

2. BX, PR and AX play 8 bars, then SX plays.

3. BX, PR, AX and SX play for 8 bars, then LD plays.

4. All instruments play ostinati for 16 bars.

5. SX plays Melody 1 twice while other instruments play ostinati to 1st Ending.

6. Go back to measure 1 and repeat same arrangement to 2nd Ending.

Level 5

1. BX, PR play 8 bars, then AX plays. (Chord changes every 4 bars.)

2. BX, PR and AX play 8 bars, then SX plays.

3. BX, PR, AX and SX play for 8 bars, then LD plays.

4. All instruments play ostinati for 16 bars.

5. SX plays Melody 1 twice while other instruments play ostinati.

6. SX plays Melody 2 four times while other instruments play ostinati to 1st Ending. (Chord changes every 2 bars.)

7. Go back to measure 1 and repeat same arrangement to 2nd Ending.

Break Ending *(Optional)*

1. Break Ending can be played at the end of all Level 1-5 arrangements.

2. Count 3 quarter notes to lead ensemble into Break Ending.

3. All instruments play Break Ending in unison.

SENEGAL

LEVEL 1 ★☆☆☆☆

CD Track: **6**

Introduce Signature Ostinato
BX, AX, SX play Signature Ostinato

SX = Soprano Xylophone
AX = Alto Xylophone
BX = Bass Xylophone
LD = Low Drum
PR = Percussion

MIYAABELE
XYLOPHONE

♩ = 130

Signature Ostinato (BX)

Traditional, arranged by Dancing Drum

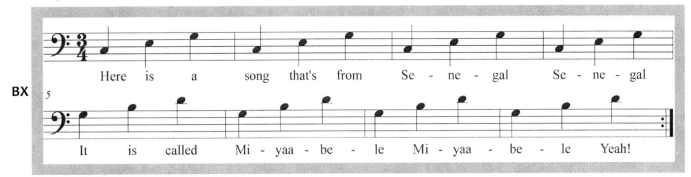

Here is a song that's from Se - ne - gal Se - ne - gal

It is called Mi - yaa - be - le Mi - yaa - be - le Yeah!

Dancing Drum © 2010

LEVEL 2 ★★☆☆☆

CD Track: **7**

Introduce AX Ostinato
BX & SX play Signature Ostinato
AX plays AX Ostinato

SX = Soprano Xylophone
AX = Alto Xylophone
BX = Bass Xylophone
LD = Low Drum
PR = Percussion

MIYAABELE
XYLOPHONE

♩ = 130

Alto Ostinato (AX)

Traditional, arranged by Dancing Drum

Mi - yaa - be - le   Mi - yaa - be - le   Mi - yaa - be - le   Mi - yaa - be - le

Is   fun   to play   Is   fun   to play   Is   fun   to play   Is   fun   to play

LEVEL 3 ★★★☆☆

CD Track: **8**

Introduce SX Ostinato
BX plays Signature Ostinato
AX plays AX Ostinato, SX plays SX Ostinato

SX = Soprano Xylophone
AX = Alto Xylophone
BX = Bass Xylophone
LD = Low Drum
PR = Percussion

MIYAABELE
XYLOPHONE

♩ = 130

Soprano Ostinato (SX)

Traditional, arranged by Dancing Drum

Dancing Drum © 2010

Introduce Melody 1 (M1)
BX plays Signature Ostinato
AX plays AX Ostinato, SX plays M1

SX = Soprano Xylophone
AX = Alto Xylophone
BX = Bass Xylophone
M1 = Melody 1

MIYAABELE
XYLOPHONE

♩ = 130

Melody 1 (M1)

Traditional, arranged by Dancing Drum

Dancing Drum © 2010

West Africa 99

Melody 1 (M1) Arrangement
Level 3 + M1 + downbeat ending

CD Track: **9**

MIYAABELE
XYLOPHONE

♩ = 130

M1 Arrangement

Traditional, arranged by Dancing Drum

Dancing Drum © 2010

MIYAABELE
XYLOPHONE

SX = Soprano Xylophone
AX = Alto Xylophone
BX = Bass Xylophone
M1 = Melody 1
LD = Low Drum
PR = Percussion

Dancing Drum © 2010

Introduce Melody 2 (M2) + M2 Ending
BX plays Signature Ostinato
AX plays AX Ostinato, SX plays M2

SX = Soprano Xylophone
AX = Alto Xylophone
BX = Bass Xylophone
M2 = Melody 1

MIYAABELE
XYLOPHONE

♩ = 130

Melody 2 (M2)

Traditional, arranged by Dancing Drum

last note of M1   **M2**   play 3x

M2 Ending

MIYAABELE

XYLOPHONE

Traditional, arranged by Dancing Drum

♩ = 130

Full Arrangement

MIYAABELE

XYLOPHONE

SX = Soprano Xylophone
AX = Alto Xylophone
BX = Bass Xylophone
M1 = Melody 1
M2 = Melody 2
LD = Low Drum
PR = Percussion

Dancing Drum © 2010

OPTIONAL: Introduce Break Ending (BE)
All instruments play BE in unison
BE can be played at any level

SX = Soprano Xylophone
AX = Alto Xylophone
BX = Bass Xylophone
LD = Low Drum
PR = Percussion
BE = Break Ending

CD Track: **11**

MIYAABELE
XYLOPHONE

♩ = 130

Break Ending (BE)

Traditional, arranged by Dancing Drum

Play the N'-Daa-ga sa-bar drum break now

Play it on your drum like you know how

Dancing Drum © 2010

Reading Connection: **Journal #4 - Labé** *(pg. 40)*
& The Balafon Story *(pg. 42)*

LAMBA

Lamba is the song of the *djeli*, or *griot*. Like many *rhythms* in West Africa, the exact origins of Lamba are unclear. Some stories say that Lamba came from a meeting of djelis during King Sundiata's reign of the *Mande* Empire, in the 13th century. At their meeting, the djelis discussed how they knew many songs, but none of the songs were especially for them. The djelis then decided to create a new rhythm, song, and dance called Lamba.

Lamba started as a tune on the *balafon*. Later, drums and other instruments were added to the music. Over time, Lamba has became a popular song performed by djelis for every occasion. In the song, the djelis give thanks for the gift of music.

Lamba is also called "Djelidon" (Dance of the Djelis).

GUINEA

A village scene in Guinea

Lamba Highlights:

Lamba is played in 4/4 time with a *"swing feel"*. It showcases the rhythms and melodies of djeli music from Guinea. The swing feel in Lamba is similar to the swing feel found in jazz music. Have your students practice swinging the 8th notes in Lamba to hear and feel the concept of swing.

♩ = 135 *Recommended Tempo*
Swing Feel

LAMBA
DRUM

SUGGESTED ARRANGEMENT

Levels 1-3

1. LD plays 8 bars , then HD plays.
2. LD and HD play 8 bars, then PR plays.
3. LD, HD, and PR play for 16 bars or as long as desired.
4. Play downbeat ending.
5. Go back to measure 1 and repeat for longer arrangement.

> **Level 1** = 1 part polyrhythm
> **Level 2** = 2 part polyrhythm
> **Level 3** = 3 part polyrhythm
> **Level 4** = 3 part polyrhythm
> + drum break

Level 4

1. Add Drum Break (DB) to beginning and end of Level 3 arrangement. All instruments play Drum Break in unison.
2. Play DB at beginning, count 4 quarter notes, and begin Level 3 arrangement. To end Level 3 arrangement, play downbeat ending, count 4 quarter notes, and finish with the final DB.

__Drum Break for Levels 1 & 2 (Optional)__ - Drum Break can also be played at the beginning and end of Level 1-2 arrangements. Level 4 = Level 3 + Drum Break.

LEARNING LEVELS

Introduce Signature Rhythm (LD)
LD, HD & PR play Signature Rhythm

Introduce HD Rhythm
LD & PR play Signature Rhythm
HD plays HD Rhythm

Introduce PR Rhythm
LD plays Signature Rhythm
HD plays HD Rhythm - PR plays PR Rhythm

Play Full Arrangement with Drum Break (DB)
DB + Level 3 + DB

OPTIONAL: Drum Break
DB can be played at any level
All instruments play DB in unison

GUINEA

LEVEL 1 ★☆☆☆

Introduce Signature Rhythm
LD, HD & PR play Signature Rhythm

CD Track: **12**

NOTATION KEY
LD = Low Drum
HD = High Drum
PR = Percussion

KEY	LOW	MID/HIGH
SOUND	Boom	Ba
SYMBOL	O	X

LAMBA
DRUM

Signature Rhythm (LD) - Rhythm Phonics

Traditional, arranged by Dancing Drum

LD

4/4	1	&	2	&	3	&	4	&	1	&	2	&	3	&	4	&
W/S	Play		Lam		ba		yeah		Play		Lam		ba		yeah	
O/X	O		O		O		X		O		O		O		X	

4/4	1	&	2	&	3	&	4	&	1	&	2	&	3	&	4	&
W/S	Play		Lam		ba		this	way	on	the		drums			yeah	
O/X	O		O		O		X	O	O	O		O			X	

W/S = Words & Syllables; **O/X** = Boom & Ba

HD

4/4	1	&	2	&	3	&	4	&	1	&	2	&	3	&	4	&
W/S	Play		Lam		ba		yeah		Play		Lam		ba		yeah	
O/X	O		O		O		X		O		O		O		X	

4/4	1	&	2	&	3	&	4	&	1	&	2	&	3	&	4	&
W/S	Play		Lam		ba		this	way	on	the		drums			yeah	
O/X	O		O		O		X	O	O	O		O			X	

PR

4/4	1	&	2	&	3	&	4	&	1	&	2	&	3	&	4	&
W/S	Play		Lam		ba		yeah		Play		Lam		ba		yeah	
O/X	X		X		X		X		X		X		X		X	

4/4	1	&	2	&	3	&	4	&	1	&	2	&	3	&	4	&
W/S	Play		Lam		ba		this	way	on	the		drums			yeah	
O/X	X		X		X		X	X	X	X		X			X	

Dancing Drum © 2010

Introduce Signature Rhythm
LD, HD, & PR play Signature Rhythm

CD Track: **12**

NOTATION KEY
LD = Low Drum
HD = High Drum
PR = Percussion

LAMBA
DRUM

♩ = 135 *Swing Feel*

Signature Rhythm (LD) - Standard Notation

Traditional, arranged by Dancing Drum

LEVEL 2 ★★☆☆

CD Track: **13**

Introduce HD Rhythm
LD & PR play Signature Rhythm
HD plays HD Rhythm

KEY	LOW	MID/HIGH
SOUND	Boom	Ba
SYMBOL	O	X

DRUM

HD Rhythm - Rhythm Phonics

Traditional, arranged by Dancing Drum

HD

4/4	1	&	2	&	3	&	4	&	1	&	2	&	3	&	4	&
W/S	Play	the	Lam	ba	now		Let's	all	play	the	Lam	ba	now		Let's	all
O/X	X	X	X	X	O		X	X	X	X	X	X	O		X	X

LD

4/4	1	&	2	&	3	&	4	&	1	&	2	&	3	&	4	&
W/S	Play		Lam		ba		yeah		Play		Lam		ba		yeah	
O/X	O		O		O		X		O		O		O		X	

4/4	1	&	2	&	3	&	4	&	1	&	2	&	3	&	4	&
W/S	Play		Lam		ba		this	way		on	the		drums		yeah	
O/X	O		O		O		X	O		O	O		O		X	

HD

4/4	1	&	2	&	3	&	4	&	1	&	2	&	3	&	4	&
W/S	Play	the	Lam	ba	now		Let's	all	play	the	Lam	ba	now		Let's	all
O/X	X	X	X	X	O		X	X	X	X	X	X	O		X	X

PR

4/4	1	&	2	&	3	&	4	&	1	&	2	&	3	&	4	&
W/S	Play		Lam		ba		yeah		Play		Lam		ba		yeah	
O/X	X		X		X		X		X		X		X		X	

4/4	1	&	2	&	3	&	4	&	1	&	2	&	3	&	4	&
W/S	Play		Lam		ba		this	way		on	the		drums		yeah	
O/X	X		X		X		X	X		X	X		X		X	

LEVEL 2

CD Track: **13**

Introduce HD Rhythm
LD & PR play Signature Rhythm
HD plays HD Rhythm

LAMBA
DRUM

♩ = 135 *Swing Feel*

HD Rhythm - Standard Notation

Traditional, arranged by Dancing Drum

Dancing Drum © 2010

LEVEL 3 ★★★☆

CD Track: **14**

Introduce PR Rhythm
LD plays Signature Rhythm
HD plays HD Rhythm - PR plays PR Rhythm

KEY	LOW	MID/HIGH
SOUND	Boom	Ba
SYMBOL	O	X

DRUM

PR Rhythm - Rhythm Phonics

Traditional, arranged by Dancing Drum

PR

4/4	1	&	2	&	3	&	4	&	1	&	2	&	3	&	4	&
W/S	This		is		Lam	ba		Play		the	beat		now			
O/X	X		X		X	X		X		X	X		X			

LD

4/4	1	&	2	&	3	&	4	&	1	&	2	&	3	&	4	&
W/S	Play		Lam		ba		yeah		Play		Lam		ba		yeah	
O/X	O		O		O		X		O		O		O		X	

4/4	1	&	2	&	3	&	4	&	1	&	2	&	3	&	4	&
W/S	Play		Lam		ba		this	way		on	the		drums		yeah	
O/X	O		O		O		X	O		O	O		O		X	

HD

4/4	1	&	2	&	3	&	4	&	1	&	2	&	3	&	4	&
W/S	Play	the	Lam	ba	now		Let's	all	play	the	Lam	ba	now		Let's	all
O/X	X	X	X	X	O		X	X	X	X	X	X	O		X	X

PR

4/4	1	&	2	&	3	&	4	&	1	&	2	&	3	&	4	&
W/S	This		is		Lam	ba		Play		the	beat		now			
O/X	X		X		X	X		X		X	X		X			

Introduce PR Rhythm
LD plays Signature Rhythm
HD plays HD Rhythm - PR plays PR Rhythm

CD Track: **14**

LAMBA
DRUM

♩ = 135 *Swing Feel*

PR Rhythm - Standard Notation

Traditional, arranged by Dancing Drum

This   is   Lam - ba   Play   the   beat   now

Dancing Drum © 2010

OPTIONAL: Drum Break
All instruments play DB in unison
DB can be played at any level

NOTATION KEY
LD = Low Drum
HD = High Drum
PR = Percussion
DB = Drum Break

CD Track: **15**

KEY	LOW	MID/HIGH
SOUND	Boom	Ba
SYMBOL	O	X

LAMBA
DRUM

Drum Break (DB) - Rhythm Phonics

Traditional, arranged by Dancing Drum

DB

4/4	1	&	2	&	3	&	4	&	1	&	2	&	3	&	4	&
W/S	It's		the	break		for	the		beat		called		Lam		ba	
O/X	X		X	X		X	X		X		O		O		O	

4/4	1	&	2	&	3	&	4	&	1	&	2	&	3	&	4	&
W/S	Let's		all	play		it		on	the		drums		now			
O/X	X		X	X		X		O	O		O		O			

Drum Break (DB) - Standard Notation

DB

It's the break for the beat called Lam - ba

3

Let's all play it on the drums now

Dancing Drum © 2010

Play Full Arrangement
DB + Level 3 + DB

LEVEL 4 ★★★★

CD Track: **16**

LAMBA
DRUM

♩ = 135 *Swing Feel*

Full Arrangement

Traditional, arranged by Dancing Drum

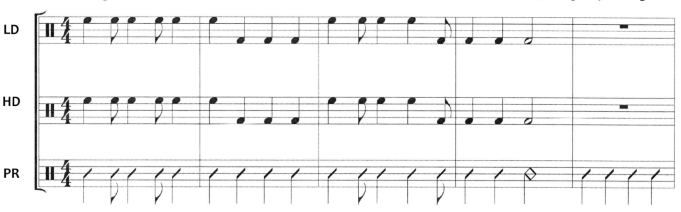

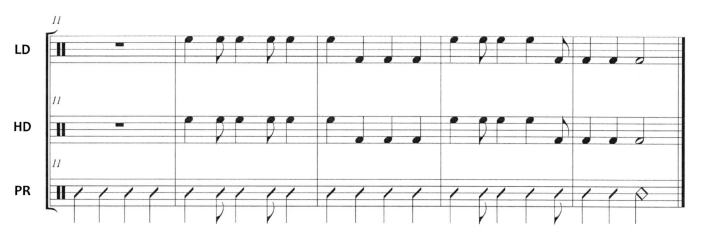

Dancing Drum © 2010

Reading Connection: **Journal #4 - Labé** (*pg. 40*)
& **The Balafon Story** (*pg. 42*)

LAMBA
XYLOPHONE

LEARNING LEVELS

LEVEL 1	★☆☆☆☆	**Introduce Signature Bass Ostinato (BX)** BX, AX, SX play Signature Ostinato
LEVEL 2	★★☆☆☆	**Introduce Alto Ostinato (AX)** BX & SX play Signature Ostinato AX plays AX Ostinato
LEVEL 3	★★★☆☆	**Introduce Soprano Ostinato (SX)** BX plays Signature Ostinato AX plays AX Ostinato, SX plays SX Ostinato
LEVEL 4	★★★★☆	**Melody 1 (M1) Arrangement** Level 3 + M1 + downbeat ending
LEVEL 5	★★★★★	**Full Arrangement** Level 3 + M1 + M2 + M2 Ending
BREAK	**Break Ending**	**OPTIONAL: Introduce Break Ending (BE)** All instruments play BE in unison BE can be played at any level

Djeli balafon player

♩ = 135 *Recommended Tempo*
Swing Feel

NOTATION KEY
SX = Soprano Xylophone
AX = Alto Xylophone
BX = Bass Xylophone
LD = Low Drum
PR = Percussion
M1 = Melody 1
M2 = Melody 2

LAMBA
XYLOPHONE

SUGGESTED ARRANGEMENT

> **Level 1** = 1 part ostinato
> **Level 2** = 2 part ostinato
> **Level 3** = 3 part ostinato
> **Level 4** = 3 part ostinato + M1
> **Level 5** = 3 part ostinato + M1 + M2

Levels 1-3

1. BX, PR play 8 bars, then AX plays.
2. BX, PR and AX play 8 bars, then SX plays.
3. BX, PR, AX, and SX play for 8 bars, then LD plays.
4. All instruments play ostinati for 16 bars or as many as desired.
5. Play downbeat ending.
6. Go back to measure 1 and repeat for longer arrangement.

Level 4

1. BX, PR play 8 bars, then AX plays.
2. BX, PR and AX play 8 bars, then SX plays.
3. BX, PR, AX and SX play for 8 bars, then LD plays.
4. All instruments play ostinati for 8 bars.
5. SX plays Melody 1 twice while other instruments play ostinati to 1st Ending.
6. Go back to measure 1 and repeat same arrangement to 2nd Ending.

Level 5

1. BX, PR play 8 bars, then AX plays.
2. BX, PR and AX play 8 bars, then SX plays.
3. BX, PR, AX and SX play for 8 bars, then LD plays.
4. All instruments play ostinati for 8 bars.
5. SX plays Melody 1 twice while other instruments play ostinati.
6. All instruments play ostinati for 8 bars.
7. SX plays Melody 2 four times while other instruments play ostinati to 1st Ending.
8. Go back to measure 1 and repeat same arrangement to 2nd Ending.

Break Ending *(Optional)*

1. Break Ending can be played at the end of all Level 1-5 arrangements.
2. Count 4 quarter notes to lead ensemble into Break Ending.
3. All instruments play Break Ending in unison.

LEVEL 1 ★☆☆☆☆

Introduce Signature Ostinato (BX)
BX, AX, SX play Signature Ostinato

CD Track: **17**

SX = Soprano Xylophone
AX = Alto Xylophone
BX = Bass Xylophone
LD = Low Drum
PR = Percussion

LAMBA
XYLOPHONE

♩ = 135 *Swing Feel*

Signature Ostinato (BX)

Traditional, arranged by Dancing Drum

LEVEL 2 ★★☆☆☆

CD Track: **18**

Introduce AX Ostinato
BX & SX play Signature Ostinato
AX plays AX Ostinato

SX = Soprano Xylophone
AX = Alto Xylophone
BX = Bass Xylophone
LD = Low Drum
PR = Percussion

LAMBA
XYLOPHONE

♩ = 135 *Swing Feel*

Alto Ostinato (AX)

Traditional, arranged by Dancing Drum

It is the song of the Dje - li It is the song of the Dje - li

Introduce SX Ostinato
BX plays Signature Ostinato
AX plays AX Ostinato, SX plays SX Ostinato

SX = Soprano Xylophone
AX = Alto Xylophone
BX = Bass Xylophone
LD = Low Drum
PR = Percussion

CD Track: **19**

LAMBA
XYLOPHONE

♩ = 135 *Swing Feel*

Soprano Ostinato (SX)

Traditional, arranged by Dancing Drum

Dancing Drum © 2010

Introduce Melody 1 (M1)
BX plays Signature Ostinato
AX plays AX Ostinato, SX plays M1

SX = Soprano Xylophone
AX = Alto Xylophone
BX = Bass Xylophone
M1 = Melody 1

LAMBA
XYLOPHONE

♩ = 135 *Swing Feel*

Melody 1 (M1)

Traditional, arranged by Dancing Drum

Melody 1 (M1) Arrangement
Level 3 + M1 + downbeat ending

SX = Soprano Xylophone
AX = Alto Xylophone
BX = Bass Xylophone
M1 = Melody 1
LD = Low Drum
PR = Percussion

LAMBA
XYLOPHONE

♩ = 135 *Swing Feel*

Traditional, arranged by Dancing Drum

M1 Arrangement

Dancing Drum © 2010

Introduce Melody 2 (M2) + M2 Ending
BX plays Signature Ostinato
AX plays AX Ostinato, SX plays M2

SX = Soprano Xylophone
AX = Alto Xylophone
BX = Bass Xylophone
M2 = Melody 1

LAMBA
XYLOPHONE

♩ = 135 *Swing Feel*

Melody 2 (M2)

Traditional, arranged by Dancing Drum

LAMBA
XYLOPHONE

Traditional, arranged by Dancing Drum

♩ = 135 *Swing Feel*

Full Arrangement

Dancing Drum © 2010

LAMBA
XYLOPHONE

SX = Soprano Xylophone
AX = Alto Xylophone
BX = Bass Xylophone
LD = Low Drum
PR = Percussion
M1 = Melody 1
M2 = Melody 2

M2 play 3x

M2 Ending

back to measure 1

Dancing Drum © 2010

BREAK **BREAK ENDING**

OPTIONAL: Introduce Break Ending (BE)
All instruments play BE in unison
BE can be played at any level

CD Track: **22**

SX = Soprano Xylophone
AX = Alto Xylophone
BX = Bass Xylophone
LD = Low Drum
PR = Percussion
BE = Break Ending

LAMBA
XYLOPHONE

♩ = 135 *Swing Feel*

Break Ending (BE)

Traditional, arranged by Dancing Drum

It's the break for the beat called Lam - ba

Let's all play it on the drums now

DIDADI

Didadi is a song, rhythm, and dance from the *Wassoulou* region of Mali. It is played to accompany Wassoulou music and for many other occasions like weddings, holidays, and welcoming guests.

Traditionally, Didadi is performed by young people at *harvest* festivals throughout Mali. Drummers play the Didadi *rhythm* on drums, and dancers compete to win the title of "Best Didadi Dancer" at the Didadi Games.

Didadi Song (in Bambara language):

*Sunguru lu ye bara da la
Yanfoyila
Awnka Didadi deonye bara da la
Ya Yanfoila*

Translation:

*We have children who have come
to the music and dancing place
for the Didadi celebration.*

Our drum and dance teachers in Mali

Didadi Highlights:

Didadi is played in 4/4 time and showcases the rhythms and *melodies* of the Wassoulou sound of Mali. The xylophone melodies are transcribed from the vocals of the Didadi song that we learned when we visited Mali.

MALI

♩ = 135 *Recommended Tempo*

DIDADI
DRUM

SUGGESTED ARRANGEMENT

| Level 1 = 1 part polyrhythm |
| Level 2 = 2 part polyrhythm |
| Level 3 = 3 part polyrhythm |
| Level 4 = 3 part polyrhythm + drum break |

Levels 1-3

1. LD plays 8 bars , then HD plays.

2. LD and HD play 8 bars, then PR plays.

3. LD, HD, and PR play for 16 bars or as long as desired.

4. Play downbeat ending.

5. Go back to measure 1 and repeat for longer arrangement.

Level 4

1. Add Drum Break (DB) to beginning and end of Level 3 arrangement. All instruments play Drum Break in unison.

2. Play DB at beginning, count 4 quarter notes, and begin Level 3 arrangement. To end Level 3 arrangement, play downbeat ending, count 4 quarter notes, and finish with the final DB.

*** Drum Break for Levels 1 & 2 (Optional)** - Drum Break can also be played at the beginning and end of Level 1-2 arrangements. Level 4 = Level 3 + Drum Break.*

LEARNING LEVELS

Introduce Signature Rhythm (LD)
LD, HD & PR play Signature Rhythm

Introduce HD Rhythm
LD & PR play Signature Rhythm
HD plays HD Rhythm

Introduce PR Rhythm
LD plays Signature Rhythm
HD plays HD Rhythm - PR plays PR Rhythm

Play Full Arrangement with Drum Break (DB)
DB + Level 3 + DB

BREAK **DRUM BREAK**

OPTIONAL: Drum Break
DB can be played at any level
All instruments play DB in unison

MALI

LEVEL 1 ★ ☆ ☆ ☆

CD Track: **23**

Introduce Signature Rhythm
LD, HD & PR play Signature Rhythm

NOTATION KEY
LD = Low Drum
HD = High Drum
PR = Percussion

KEY	LOW	MID/HIGH
SOUND	Boom	Ba
SYMBOL	O	X

DRUM

Signature Rhythm (LD) - Rhythm Phonics

Traditional, arranged by Dancing Drum

LD	4/4	1	&	2	&	3	&	4	&	1	&	2	&	3	&	4	&
	W/S	Now		let's	play		Di	da		di		on		the		drums	
	O/X	O		X	X		X	X		X		O		X		X	

W/S = Words & Syllables; **O/X** = Boom & Ba

LD	4/4	1	&	2	&	3	&	4	&	1	&	2	&	3	&	4	&
	W/S	Now		let's	play		Di	da		di		on		the		drums	
	O/X	O		X	X		X	X		X		O		X		X	

HD	4/4	1	&	2	&	3	&	4	&	1	&	2	&	3	&	4	&
	W/S	Now		let's	play		Di	da		di		on		the		drums	
	O/X	O		X	X		X	X		X		O		X		X	

PR	4/4	1	&	2	&	3	&	4	&	1	&	2	&	3	&	4	&
	W/S	Now		let's	play		Di	da		di		on		the		drums	
	O/X	X		X	X		X	X		X		X		X		X	

LEVEL 1 ★☆☆☆

CD Track: **23**

Introduce Signature Rhythm
LD, HD, & PR play Signature Rhythm

DIDADI
DRUM

♩ = 135

Signature Rhythm (LD) - Standard Notation

Traditional, arranged by Dancing Drum

Now   let's   play   Di - da - di   on   the   drums

LEVEL 2 ★★☆☆

CD Track: **24**

KEY	LOW	MID/HIGH
SOUND	Boom	Ba
SYMBOL	O	X

Introduce HD Rhythm
LD & PR play Signature Rhythm
HD plays HD Rhythm

NOTATION KEY
LD = Low Drum
HD = High Drum
PR = Percussion

DIDADI
DRUM

HD Rhythm - Rhythm Phonics

Traditional, arranged by Dancing Drum

	4/4	1	&	2	&	3	&	4	&	1	&	2	&	3	&	4	&
HD	W/S	Play			the	beat		Play	the	Di			da	di		Yeah!	
	O/X	X			X	X		X	X	X			X	X		O	

	4/4	1	&	2	&	3	&	4	&	1	&	2	&	3	&	4	&
LD	W/S	Now		let's	play		Di	da		di		on		the		drums	
	O/X	O		X	X		X	X		X		O		X		X	

	4/4	1	&	2	&	3	&	4	&	1	&	2	&	3	&	4	&
HD	W/S	Play			the	beat		Play	the	Di			da	di		Yeah!	
	O/X	X			X	X		X	X	X			X	X		O	

	4/4	1	&	2	&	3	&	4	&	1	&	2	&	3	&	4	&
PR	W/S	Now		let's	play		Di	da		di		on		the		drums	
	O/X	X		X	X		X	X		X		X		X		X	

LEVEL 2 ★★☆☆

CD Track: **24**

Introduce HD Rhythm
LD & PR play Signature Rhythm
HD plays HD Rhythm

DIDADI
DRUM

♩ = 135

HD Rhythm - Standard Notation

Traditional, arranged by Dancing Drum

LEVEL 3 ★★★☆

CD Track: **25**

Introduce PR Rhythm
LD plays Signature Rhythm
HD plays HD Rhythm - PR plays PR Rhythm

KEY	LOW	MID/HIGH
SOUND	Boom	Ba
SYMBOL	O	X

DRUM

PR Rhythm - Rhythm Phonics

Traditional, arranged by Dancing Drum

PR

4/4	1	&	2	&	3	&	4	&	1	&	2	&	3	&	4	&
W/S	Here	is			the	beat			called		Di		da	di		
O/X	X	X			X	X			X		X		X	X		

LD

4/4	1	&	2	&	3	&	4	&	1	&	2	&	3	&	4	&
W/S	Now		let's	play		Di	da		di		on		the		drums	
O/X	O		X	X		X	X		X		O		X		X	

HD

4/4	1	&	2	&	3	&	4	&	1	&	2	&	3	&	4	&
W/S	Play			the	beat		Play	the	Di			da	di		Yeah!	
O/X	X			X	X		X	X	X			X	X		O	

PR

4/4	1	&	2	&	3	&	4	&	1	&	2	&	3	&	4	&
W/S	Here	is			the	beat			called		Di		da	di		
O/X	X	X			X	X			X		X		X	X		

Introduce PR Rhythm
LD plays Signature Rhythm
HD plays HD Rhythm - PR plays PR Rhythm

CD Track: **25**

NOTATION KEY
LD = Low Drum
HD = High Drum
PR = Percussion

DIDADI
DRUM

♩ = 135

PR Rhythm - Standard Notation

Traditional, arranged by Dancing Drum

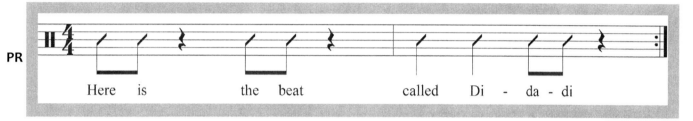

 **DRUM BREAK**

OPTIONAL: Drum Break
All instruments play DB in unison
DB can be played at any level

NOTATION KEY
LD = Low Drum
HD = High Drum
PR = Percussion
DB = Drum Break

CD Track: **26**

KEY	LOW	MID/HIGH
SOUND	Boom	Ba
SYMBOL	O	X

DIDADI
DRUM

Drum Break (DB) - Rhythm Phonics

Traditional, arranged by Dancing Drum

DB

4/4	1	&	2	&	3	&	4	&	1	&	2	&	3	&	4	&
W/S	Let's	all		play		the		break	for		Di		da		di	
O/X	X	O		O		O		O	X		O		O		O	

4/4	1	&	2	&	3	&	4	&	1	&	2	&	3	&	4	&
W/S	Here	we	go	now	Here	we	go	now	Play	Di		da	di			
O/X	O	O	O	O	O	O	O	O	X	X		X	X			

Drum Break (DB) - Standard Notation

DB

Play Full Arrangement
DB + Level 3 + DB

NOTATION KEY
LD = Low Drum
HD = High Drum
PR = Percussion
DB = Drum Break

CD Track: **27**

DIDADI
DRUM

♩ = 135

Full Arrangement

Traditional, arranged by Dancing Drum

Dancing Drum © 2010

DIDADI
XYLOPHONE

LEARNING LEVELS

Introduce Signature Bass Ostinato (BX)
BX, AX, SX play Signature Ostinato

Introduce Alto Ostinato (AX)
BX & SX play Signature Ostinato
AX plays AX Ostinato

Introduce Soprano Ostinato (SX)
BX plays Signature Ostinato
AX plays AX Ostinato, SX plays SX Ostinato

Melody 1 (M1) Arrangement
Level 3 + M1 + downbeat ending

Full Arrangement
Level 3 + M1 + M2 + M2 Ending

OPTIONAL: Introduce Break Ending (BE)
All instruments play BE in unison
BE can be played at any level

Wassoulou singer, Oumou Sangare

♩ = 135 *Recommended Tempo*

SX = Soprano Xylophone
AX = Alto Xylophone
BX = Bass Xylophone
LD = Low Drum
PR = Percussion
M1 = Melody 1
M2 = Melody 2

DIDADI
XYLOPHONE

SUGGESTED ARRANGEMENT

> **Level 1** = 1 part ostinato
> **Level 2** = 2 part ostinato
> **Level 3** = 3 part ostinato
> **Level 4** = 3 part ostinato + M1
> **Level 5** = 3 part ostinato + M1 + M2

Levels 1-3

1. BX, PR play 8 bars, then AX plays.
2. BX, PR and AX play 8 bars, then SX plays.
3. BX, PR, AX, and SX play for 8 bars, then LD plays.
4. All instruments play ostinati for 16 bars or as many as desired.
5. Play downbeat ending.
6. Go back to measure 1 and repeat for longer arrangement.

Level 4

1. BX, PR play 8 bars, then AX plays.
2. BX, PR and AX play 8 bars, then SX plays.
3. BX, PR, AX and SX play for 8 bars, then LD plays.
4. All instruments play ostinati for 8 bars.
5. SX plays Melody 1 twice while other instruments play ostinati to 1st Ending.
6. Go back to measure 1 and repeat same arrangement to 2nd Ending.

Level 5

1. BX, PR play 8 bars, then AX plays.
2. BX, PR and AX play 8 bars, then SX plays.
3. BX, PR, AX and SX play for 8 bars, then LD plays.
4. All instruments play ostinati for 8 bars.
5. SX plays Melody 1 twice while other instruments play ostinati.
6. All instruments play ostinati for 8 bars.
7. SX plays Melody 2 four times while other instruments play ostinati to 1st Ending.
8. Repeat same arrangement to 2nd Ending.

Break Ending *(Optional)*

1. Break Ending can be played at the end of all Level 1-5 arrangements.
2. Count 4 quarter notes to lead ensemble into Break Ending.
3. All instruments play Break Ending in unison.

Introduce Signature Ostinato (BX)
BX, AX, SX play Signature Ostinato

SX = Soprano Xylophone
AX = Alto Xylophone
BX = Bass Xylophone
LD = Low Drum
PR = Percussion

DIDADI
XYLOPHONE

♩ = 135

Signature Ostinato (BX)

Traditional, arranged by Dancing Drum

Now   let's   play   Di - da - di   on   the   drums

Dancing Drum © 2010

Introduce AX Ostinato
BX & SX play Signature Ostinato
AX plays AX Ostinato

SX = Soprano Xylophone
AX = Alto Xylophone
BX = Bass Xylophone
LD = Low Drum
PR = Percussion

CD Track: **29**

XYLOPHONE

♩ = 135

Alto Ostinato (AX)

Traditional, arranged by Dancing Drum

Here is the Di - da - di   from the coun - try   Ma - li

LEVEL 3 ★★★☆☆

CD Track: **30**

Introduce SX Ostinato
BX plays Signature Ostinato
AX plays AX Ostinato, SX plays SX Ostinato

SX = Soprano Xylophone
AX = Alto Xylophone
BX = Bass Xylophone
LD = Low Drum
PR = Percussion

DIDADI
XYLOPHONE

♩ = 135

Soprano Ostinato (SX)

Traditional, arranged by Dancing Drum

Lis - ten   to the Di - da - di   Now let's all

Introduce Melody 1 (M1)
BX plays Signature Ostinato
AX plays AX Ostinato, SX plays M1

SX = Soprano Xylophone
AX = Alto Xylophone
BX = Bass Xylophone
M1 = Melody 1

XYLOPHONE

♩ = 135

Melody 1 (M1)

Traditional, arranged by Dancing Drum

pickup note for M1

Dancing Drum © 2010

LEVEL 4 ★★★★☆

CD Track: **31**

Melody 1 (M1) Arrangement
Level 3 + M1 + downbeat ending

SX = Soprano Xylophone
AX = Alto Xylophone
BX = Bass Xylophone
M1 = Melody 1
LD = Low Drum
PR = Percussion

DIDADI
XYLOPHONE

♩ = 135

M1 Arrangement

Traditional, arranged by Dancing Drum

pickup note for M1

back to measure 1

M1   play 2x

Dancing Drum © 2010

Introduce Melody 2 (M2) + M2 Ending
BX plays Signature Ostinato
AX plays AX Ostinato, SX plays M2

SX = Soprano Xylophone
AX = Alto Xylophone
BX = Bass Xylophone
M2 = Melody 1

DIDADI
XYLOPHONE

♩ = 135

Melody 2 (M2)

Traditional, arranged by Dancing Drum

Full Arrangement
Level 3 + M1 + M2 + M2 Ending

CD Track: **32**

DIDADI

♩ = 135

Full Arrangement

Traditional, arranged by Dancing Drum

DIDADI
XYLOPHONE

Dancing Drum © 2010

BREAK **BREAK ENDING**

CD Track: **33**

OPTIONAL: Introduce Break Ending (BE)
All instruments play BE in unison
BE can be played at any level

SX = Soprano Xylophone
AX = Alto Xylophone
BX = Bass Xylophone
LD = Low Drum
PR = Percussion
BE = Break Ending

DIDADI
XYLOPHONE

♩ = 135

Break Ending (BE)

Traditional, arranged by Dancing Drum

BE

Let's all play the break for Di - da - di
here we go now here we go now play Di - da - di

SX

AX

BX

LD

PR

Dancing Drum © 2010

TAKAMBA

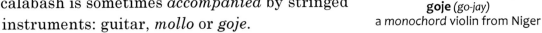

Takamba is a style of rhythm and dance performed by the *Tuareg* and *Songhai* people of Niger and Mali. The word Takamba comes from an abbreviated version of the Songhai phrase, *"Ganu ma<u>te</u> <u>kan</u> ni ga <u>ba</u>,"* which translates to, "Dance the way you like to dance."

Takamba features a graceful dance performed by men and women, seated or standing. The dance is characterized by slow, wave-like movements of the shoulders and arms from right to left. As they move their arms, the dancers roll their eyes in a sweet, playful way.

The movements of the dance are driven by the beat of a *calabash* drum, or *gasu*, which is played with hands covered in rings. Striking the rounded bottom of the gasu with the heel of the hand creates a powerful boom sound. In contrast, the metal rings worn on each finger clack on the surface of the dried *gourd*. Together, these two sounds create a rhythmic effect of galloping horses or camels. The calabash is sometimes *accompanied* by stringed instruments: guitar, *mollo* or *goje*.

goje (*go-jay*)
a monochord violin from Niger

gasu (*gah-soo*) player, Boubacar Souleyman,
with silver rings on his fingers

Takamba Highlights:

Takamba is played in 6/8 time and showcases the *rhythms* and melodies of Niger. The feel of Takamba resembles the graceful, flowing dance that it accompanies. The Signature Rhythm is derived from beat of the *gasu*, and the Soprano Xylophone Ostinato is inspired by the haunting melodies of the *goje* violin played in Takamba music.

NIGER

♩. = 96 *Recommended Tempo*

TAKAMBA
DRUM

SUGGESTED ARRANGEMENT

Levels 1-3

1. LD plays 8 bars , then HD plays.
2. LD and HD play 8 bars, then PR plays.
3. LD, HD, and PR play for 16 bars or as long as desired.
4. Play downbeat ending.
5. Go back to measure 1 and repeat for longer arrangement.

> **Level 1** = 1 part polyrhythm
> **Level 2** = 2 part polyrhythm
> **Level 3** = 3 part polyrhythm
> **Level 4** = 3 part polyrhythm
> + drum break

Level 4

1. Add Drum Break (DB) to beginning and end of Level 3 arrangement. All instruments play Drum Break in unison.
2. Play DB at beginning, count 3 quarter notes, and begin Level 3 arrangement. To end Level 3 arrangement, play downbeat ending, count 3 quarter notes, and finish with the final DB.

* Drum Break for Levels 1 & 2 (Optional) - Drum Break can also be played at the beginning and end of Level 1-2 arrangements. Level 4 = Level 3 + Drum Break.

NIGER

LEARNING LEVELS

LEVEL 1 ★☆☆☆ **Introduce Signature Rhythm (LD)**
LD, HD & PR play Signature Rhythm

LEVEL 2 ★★☆☆ **Introduce HD Rhythm**
LD & PR play Signature Rhythm
HD plays HD Rhythm

LEVEL 3 ★★★☆ **Introduce PR Rhythm**
LD plays Signature Rhythm
HD plays HD Rhythm - PR plays PR Rhythm

LEVEL 4 ★★★★ **Play Full Arrangement with Drum Break (DB)**
DB + Level 3 + DB

BREAK **DRUM BREAK** **OPTIONAL: Drum Break**
DB can be played at any level
All instruments play DB in unison

LEVEL 1 ★☆☆☆

Introduce Signature Rhythm
LD, HD & PR play Signature Rhythm

CD Track: **34**

NOTATION KEY
LD = Low Drum
HD = High Drum
PR = Percussion

KEY	LOW	MID/HIGH
SOUND	Boom	Ba
SYMBOL	O	X

TAKAMBA
DRUM

Signature Rhythm (LD) - Rhythm Phonics

Traditional, arranged by Dancing Drum

LD

6/8	1	2	3	4	5	6	1	2	3	4	5	6
W/S	Let's		play			Ta	kam		ba			like
O/X	O		O			O	O		O			O

6/8	1	2	3	4	5	6	1	2	3	4	5	6
W/S	this				play	Ta	kam		ba			now
O/X	O				X	X	X		X			O

W/S = Words & Syllables; O/X = Boom & Ba

HD

6/8	1	2	3	4	5	6	1	2	3	4	5	6
W/S	Let's		play			Ta	kam		ba			like
O/X	O		O			O	O		O			O

6/8	1	2	3	4	5	6	1	2	3	4	5	6
W/S	this				play	Ta	kam		ba			now
O/X	O				X	X	X		X			O

PR

6/8	1	2	3	4	5	6	1	2	3	4	5	6
W/S	Let's		play			Ta	kam		ba			like
O/X	X		X			X	X		X			X

6/8	1	2	3	4	5	6	1	2	3	4	5	6
W/S	this				play	Ta	kam		ba			now
O/X	X				X	X	X		X			X

Dancing Drum © 2010

LEVEL 1 ★☆☆☆

CD Track: **34**

Introduce Signature Rhythm
LD, HD, & PR play Signature Rhythm

NOTATION KEY
LD = Low Drum
HD = High Drum
PR = Percussion

TAKAMBA
DRUM

♩. = 96

Signature Rhythm (LD) - Standard Notation

Traditional, arranged by Dancing Drum

LEVEL 2 ★★☆☆

CD Track: **35**

Introduce HD Rhythm
LD & PR play Signature Rhythm
HD plays HD Rhythm

LD = Low Drum
HD = High Drum
PR = Percussion

KEY	LOW	MID/HIGH
SOUND	Boom	Ba
SYMBOL	O	X

TAKAMBA
DRUM

HD Rhythm - Rhythm Phonics

Traditional, arranged by Dancing Drum

HD

6/8	1	2	3	4	5	6	1	2	3	4	5	6
W/S	Play		Ta	kam	ba		play		Ta	kam	ba	
O/X	O		X	X	X		O		X	X	X	

W/S = Words & Syllables; O/X = Boom & Ba

LD

6/8	1	2	3	4	5	6	1	2	3	4	5	6
W/S	let's		play			Ta	kam		ba			like
O/X	O		O			O	O		O			O

6/8	1	2	3	4	5	6	1	2	3	4	5	6
W/S	this				play	Ta	kam		ba			now
O/X	O				X	X	X		X			O

HD

6/8	1	2	3	4	5	6	1	2	3	4	5	6
W/S	Play		Ta	kam	ba		play		Ta	kam	ba	
O/X	O		X	X	X		O		X	X	X	

PR

6/8	1	2	3	4	5	6	1	2	3	4	5	6
W/S	let's		play			Ta	kam		ba			like
O/X	X		X			X	X		X			X

6/8	1	2	3	4	5	6	1	2	3	4	5	6
W/S	this				play	Ta	kam		ba			now
O/X	X				X	X	X		X			X

Dancing Drum © 2010

LEVEL 2 ★★☆☆

CD Track: **35**

Introduce HD Rhythm
LD & PR play Signature Rhythm
HD plays HD Rhythm

TAKAMBA
DRUM

♩. = 96

HD Rhythm - Standard Notation

Traditional, arranged by Dancing Drum

Dancing Drum © 2010

CD Track: **36**

Introduce PR Rhythm
LD plays Signature Rhythm
HD plays HD Rhythm - PR plays PR Rhythm

NOTATION KEY
LD = Low Drum
HD = High Drum
PR = Percussion

KEY	LOW	MID/HIGH
SOUND	Boom	Ba
SYMBOL	O	X

TAKAMBA
DRUM

PR Rhythm - Rhythm Phonics

Traditional, arranged by Dancing Drum

PR

6/8	1	2	3	4	5	6	1	2	3	4	5	6
W/S	Ta		kam		ba		is	the		beat		the
O/X	X		X		X		X	X		X		X

W/S = Words & Syllables; **O/X** = Boom & Ba

LD

6/8	1	2	3	4	5	6	1	2	3	4	5	6
W/S	let's		play			Ta	kam		ba			like
O/X	O		O			O	O		O			O

6/8	1	2	3	4	5	6	1	2	3	4	5	6
W/S	this				play	Ta	kam		ba			now
O/X	O				X	X	X		X			O

HD

6/8	1	2	3	4	5	6	1	2	3	4	5	6
W/S	Play		Ta	kam	ba		play		Ta	kam	ba	
O/X	O		X	X	X		O		X	X	X	

PR

6/8	1	2	3	4	5	6	1	2	3	4	5	6
W/S	Ta		kam		ba		is	the		beat		the
O/X	X		X		X		X	X		X		X

Dancing Drum © 2010

LEVEL 3

CD Track: **36**

Introduce PR Rhythm
LD plays Signature Rhythm
HD plays HD Rhythm - PR plays PR Rhythm

NOTATION KEY
LD = Low Drum
HD = High Drum
PR = Percussion

♩. = 96

TAKAMBA
DRUM

PR Rhythm - Standard Notation

Traditional, arranged by Dancing Drum

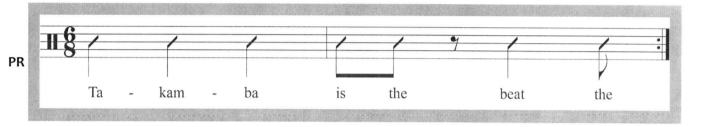

OPTIONAL: Drum Break
All instruments play DB in unison
DB can be played at any level

CD Track: **37**

KEY	LOW	MID/HIGH
SOUND	Boom	Ba
SYMBOL	O	X

TAKAMBA
DRUM

Drum Break (DB) - Rhythm Phonics

Traditional, arranged by Dancing Drum

DB

6/8	1	2	3	4	5	6	1	2	3	4	5	6	1	2	3	4	5	6
W/S	It	is	the	break	for		Ta		kam		ba		It	is	the	break	for	
O/X	X	X	X	X	X		O		O		O		X	X	X	X	X	

6/8	1	2	3	4	5	6	1	2	3	4	5	6	1	2	3	4	5	6
W/S	Ta		kam		ba		Play	it	for	Ta	kam	ba	now					
O/X	O		O		O		O	O	O	O	O	O	X					

Drum Break (DB) - Standard Notation

DB

It is the break for Ta - kam - ba It is the break for

Ta - kam - ba Play it for Ta - kam - ba now

Dancing Drum © 2010

Play Full Arrangement
DB + Level 3 + DB

LEVEL 4 ★★★★

CD Track: **38**

♩. = 96

TAKAMBA
DRUM

Full Arrangement

Traditional, arranged by Dancing Drum

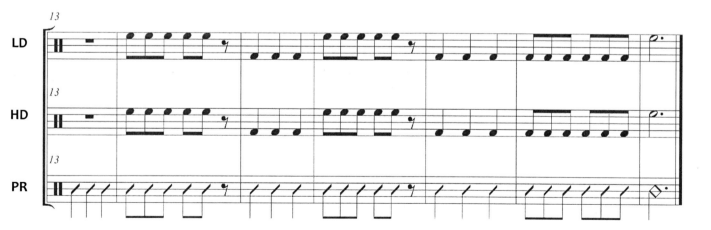

TAKAMBA
XYLOPHONE

LEARNING LEVELS

LEVEL 1 ★☆☆☆☆   **Introduce Signature Bass Ostinato (BX)**
BX, AX, SX play Signature Ostinato

LEVEL 2 ★★☆☆☆   **Introduce Alto Ostinato (AX)**
BX & SX play Signature Ostinato
AX plays AX Ostinato

LEVEL 3 ★★★☆☆   **Introduce Soprano Ostinato (SX)**
BX plays Signature Ostinato
AX plays AX Ostinato, SX plays SX Ostinato

LEVEL 4 ★★★★☆   **Melody 1 (M1) Arrangement**
Level 3 + M1 + downbeat ending

LEVEL 5 ★★★★★   **Full Arrangement**
Level 3 + M1 + M2 + M2 Ending

BREAK **BREAK ENDING**   **OPTIONAL: Introduce Break Ending (BE)**
All instruments play BE in unison
BE can be played at any level

Nigerien Afropop group Mamar Kassey
performing a Takamba song and dance

♩. = 96 *Recommended Tempo*

NOTATION KEY
SX = Soprano Xylophone
AX = Alto Xylophone
BX = Bass Xylophone
LD = Low Drum
PR = Percussion
M1 = Melody 1
M2 = Melody 2

TAKAMBA
XYLOPHONE

SUGGESTED ARRANGEMENT

> **Level 1** = 1 part ostinato
> **Level 2** = 2 part ostinato
> **Level 3** = 3 part ostinato
> **Level 4** = 3 part ostinato + M1
> **Level 5** = 3 part ostinato + M1 + M2

Levels 1-3

1. BX, PR play 8 bars, then AX plays.
2. BX, PR and AX play 8 bars, then SX plays.
3. BX, PR, AX, and SX play for 8 bars, then LD plays.
4. All instruments play ostinati for 16 bars or as many as desired.
5. Play downbeat ending.
6. Go back to measure 1 and repeat for longer arrangement.

Level 4

1. BX, PR play 8 bars, then AX plays.
2. BX, PR and AX play 8 bars, then SX plays.
3. BX, PR, AX and SX play for 8 bars, then LD plays.
4. All instruments play ostinati for 16 bars.
5. SX plays Melody 1 twice while other instruments play ostinati to 1st Ending.
6. Go back to measure 1 and repeat same arrangement to 2nd Ending.

Level 5

1. BX, PR play 8 bars, then AX plays.
2. BX, PR and AX play 8 bars, then SX plays.
3. BX, PR, AX and SX play for 8 bars, then LD plays.
4. All instruments play ostinati for 16 bars.
5. SX plays Melody 1 twice while other instruments play ostinati.
6. SX plays Melody 2 four times while other instruments play ostinati to 1st Ending.
7. Go back to measure 1 and repeat same arrangement to 2nd Ending.

Break Ending *(Optional)*

1. Break Ending can be played at the end of all Level 1-5 arrangements.
2. Count 3 quarter notes to lead ensemble into Break Ending.
3. All instruments play Break Ending in unison.

LEVEL 1 ★☆☆☆☆

CD Track: **39**

Introduce Signature Ostinato (BX)
BX, AX, SX play Signature Ostinato

SX = Soprano Xylophone
AX = Alto Xylophone
BX = Bass Xylophone
LD = Low Drum
PR = Percussion

TAKAMBA
XYLOPHONE

♩. = 96

Signature Ostinato (BX)

Traditional, arranged by Dancing Drum

BX
Let's play Ta - kam - ba like this Play Ta - kam - ba Now

Introduce AX Ostinato
BX & SX play Signature Ostinato
AX plays AX Ostinato

SX = Soprano Xylophone
AX = Alto Xylophone
BX = Bass Xylophone
LD = Low Drum
PR = Percussion

CD Track: **40**

TAKAMBA
XYLOPHONE

♩. = 96

Alto Ostinato (AX)

Traditional, arranged by Dancing Drum

Introduce SX Ostinato
BX plays Signature Ostinato
AX plays AX Ostinato, SX plays SX Ostinato

CD Track: **41**

SX = Soprano Xylophone
AX = Alto Xylophone
BX = Bass Xylophone
LD = Low Drum
PR = Percussion

TAKAMBA
XYLOPHONE

♩. = 96

Soprano Ostinato (SX)

Traditional, arranged by Dancing Drum

Lis - ten to the Ta - kam - ba   Play   the song from the   Sa - ha - ra

Dancing Drum © 2010

Introduce Melody 1 (M1)
BX plays Signature Ostinato
AX plays AX Ostinato, SX plays M1

SX = Soprano Xylophone
AX = Alto Xylophone
BX = Bass Xylophone
M1 = Melody 1

TAKAMBA
XYLOPHONE

♩. = 96

Melody 1 (M1)

Traditional, arranged by Dancing Drum

Dancing Drum © 2010

SX = Soprano Xylophone
AX = Alto Xylophone
BX = Bass Xylophone
M1 = Melody 1
LD = Low Drum
PR = Percussion

LEVEL 4 ★★★★☆   **Melody 1 (M1) Arrangement**
Level 3 + M1 + downbeat ending

CD Track: **42**

TAKAMBA
XYLOPHONE

Traditional, arranged by Dancing Drum

♩. = 96

M1 Arrangement

Introduce Melody 2 (M2) + M2 Ending
BX plays Signature Ostinato
AX plays AX Ostinato, SX plays M2

SX = Soprano Xylophone
AX = Alto Xylophone
BX = Bass Xylophone
M2 = Melody 1

TAKAMBA
XYLOPHONE

♩. = 96

Melody 2 (M2)

Traditional, arranged by Dancing Drum

LEVEL 5 ★★★★★

Full Arrangement
Level 3 + M1 + M2 + M2 Ending

CD Track: **43**

TAKAMBA
XYLOPHONE

♩. = 96

Full Arrangement

Traditional, arranged by Dancing Drum

Dancing Drum © 2010

TAKAMBA
XYLOPHONE

Dancing Drum © 2010

BREAK | **BREAK ENDING**

CD Track: **44**

OPTIONAL: Introduce Break Ending (BE)
All instruments play BE in unison
BE can be played at any level

SX = Soprano Xylophone
AX = Alto Xylophone
BX = Bass Xylophone
LD = Low Drum
PR = Percussion
BE = Break Ending

TAKAMBA
XYLOPHONE

♩. = 96

Break Ending (BE)

Traditional, arranged by Dancing Drum

It is the break for Ta - kam - ba It is the break for
Ta - kam - ba Play it for Ta - kam - ba now

Dancing Drum © 2010

MAKOSSA

▪▫▪▫▫▪▫▪▫▫▪▫▪▫▪▫▪▫▫▪▫▪▫▪▫▪▫▪▫▫▪▫▪▫▪▫▪▫▫▪▫▪▫▪▫▫▪▫

Makossa is a celebration rhythm played in Burkina Faso. Its purpose is to make people dance and have fun.

The song that we were taught for Makossa is about a dancer named Aisha. In the Jula language, the song goes like this:

Makossa Song

Oh wey, Oh wey!
Oh wey, Oh wey!
An ka mogo lo
Aisha!
A bi se dona
Aisha!

Translation

Oh wey, Oh wey!
Oh wey, Oh wey!
Come to our place,
Aisha!
She really knows how to dance,
Aisha!

Performing group, Lilidya, in Bobo-Dioulasso, Burkina Faso. The name "Lilidya" means "deep roots" in the Jula language.

Makossa Highlights:

Makossa is played in 4/4 time and is felt in 2, with the half note getting the beat. The xylophone melodies are transcribed from the vocals of the Makossa song that we learned when visiting Bobo-Dioulasso. The ♩. ♩. ♩ pattern found several times throughout Makossa is an excellent example of the rhythm and feel of Burkina Faso's musical style.

BURKINA FASO

♩ = 105 *Recommended Tempo*
Feel in 2

NOTATION KEY
LD = Low Drum
HD = High Drum
PR = Percussion
DB = Drum Break

MAKOSSA
DRUM

SUGGESTED ARRANGEMENT

Levels 1-3

> **Level 1** = 1 part polyrhythm
> **Level 2** = 2 part polyrhythm
> **Level 3** = 3 part polyrhythm
> **Level 4** = 3 part polyrhythm
>   + drum break

1. LD plays 8 bars , then HD plays.

2. LD and HD play 8 bars, then PR plays.

3. LD, HD, and PR play for 16 bars or as long as desired.

4. Play downbeat ending.

5. Go back to measure 1 and repeat for longer arrangement.

Level 4

1. Add Drum Break (DB) to beginning and end of Level 3 arrangement. All instruments play Drum Break in unison.

2. Play DB at beginning, count 4 half notes, and begin Level 3 arrangement. To end Level 3 arrangement, play downbeat ending, count 4 half notes, and finish with the final DB.

*** Drum Break for Levels 1 & 2 (Optional)** - Drum Break can also be played at the beginning and end of Level 1-2 arrangements. Level 4 = Level 3 + Drum Break.*

LEARNING LEVELS

Introduce Signature Rhythm (LD)
LD, HD & PR play Signature Rhythm

Introduce HD Rhythm
LD & PR play Signature Rhythm
HD plays HD Rhythm

Introduce PR Rhythm
LD plays Signature Rhythm
HD plays HD Rhythm - PR plays PR Rhythm

LEVEL 4 ★★★★
Play Full Arrangement with Drum Break (DB)
DB + Level 3 + DB

BREAK **DRUM BREAK**
OPTIONAL: Drum Break
DB can be played at any level
All instruments play DB in unison

BURKINA FASO

Introduce Signature Rhythm
LD, HD & PR play Signature Rhythm

KEY	LOW	MID/HIGH
SOUND	Boom	Ba
SYMBOL	O	X

MAKOSSA
DRUM

Signature Rhythm (LD) - Rhythm Phonics

Traditional, arranged by Dancing Drum

	4/4	1	&	2	&	3	&	4	&	1	&	2	&	3	&	4	&
LD	W/S	This			song			is		Ma		kos		sa			
	O/X	O			O			X		O		O		X			

W/S = Words & Syllables; **O/X** = Boom & Ba

	4/4	1	&	2	&	3	&	4	&	1	&	2	&	3	&	4	&
LD	W/S	This			song			is		Ma		kos		sa			
	O/X	O			O			X		O		O		X			

	4/4	1	&	2	&	3	&	4	&	1	&	2	&	3	&	4	&
HD	W/S	This			song			is		Ma		kos		sa			
	O/X	O			O			X		O		O		X			

	4/4	1	&	2	&	3	&	4	&	1	&	2	&	3	&	4	&
PR	W/S	This			song			is		Ma		kos		sa			
	O/X	X			X			X		X		X		X			

CD Track: **45**

Introduce Signature Rhythm
LD, HD, & PR play Signature Rhythm

NOTATION KEY
LD = Low Drum
HD = High Drum
PR = Percussion

MAKOSSA
DRUM

♩ = 105 *Feel in 2*

Signature Rhythm (LD) - Standard Notation

Traditional, arranged by Dancing Drum

LEVEL 2 ★★☆☆

CD Track: **46**

Introduce HD Rhythm
LD & PR play Signature Rhythm
HD plays HD Rhythm

NOTATION KEY
LD = Low Drum
HD = High Drum
PR = Percussion

KEY	LOW	MID/HIGH
SOUND	Boom	Ba
SYMBOL	O	X

MAKOSSA
DRUM

HD Rhythm - Rhythm Phonics

Traditional, arranged by Dancing Drum

HD	4/4	1	&	2	&	3	&	4	&	1	&	2	&	3	&	4	&
	W/S	Play			the	beat		we		call		Ma		kos	sa		
	O/X	O			X	O		X		O		X		X	X		

LD	4/4	1	&	2	&	3	&	4	&	1	&	2	&	3	&	4	&
	W/S	This		song				is		Ma		kos		sa			
	O/X	O		O				X		O		O		X			

HD	4/4	1	&	2	&	3	&	4	&	1	&	2	&	3	&	4	&
	W/S	Play			the	beat		we		call		Ma		kos	sa		
	O/X	O			X	O		X		O		X		X	X		

PR	4/4	1	&	2	&	3	&	4	&	1	&	2	&	3	&	4	&
	W/S	This		song				is		Ma		kos		sa			
	O/X	X		X				X		X		X		X			

CD Track: **46**

Introduce HD Rhythm
LD & PR play Signature Rhythm
HD plays HD Rhythm

NOTATION KEY
LD = Low Drum
HD = High Drum
PR = Percussion

MAKOSSA
DRUM

♩ = 105 *Feel in 2*

HD Rhythm - Standard Notation

Traditional, arranged by Dancing Drum

Play   the   beat   we   call   Ma - kos - sa

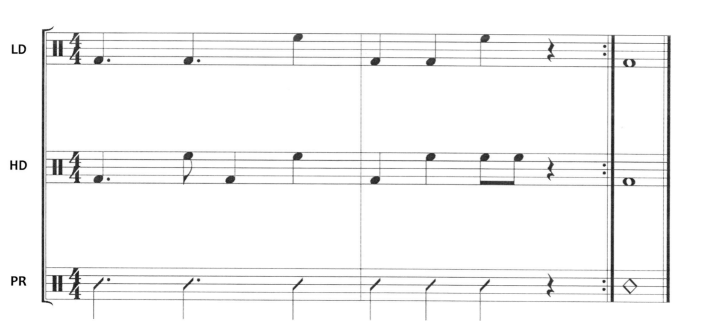

Introduce PR Rhythm
LD plays Signature Rhythm
HD plays HD Rhythm - PR plays PR Rhythm

NOTATION KEY
LD = Low Drum
HD = High Drum
PR = Percussion

KEY	LOW	MID/HIGH
SOUND	Boom	Ba
SYMBOL	O	X

DRUM

PR Rhythm - Rhythm Phonics

Traditional, arranged by Dancing Drum

PR

4/4	1	&	2	&	3	&	4	&	1	&	2	&	3	&	4	&
W/S	Play			the			rhy	thm			like		this			
O/X	X			X			X	X			X		X			

LD

4/4	1	&	2	&	3	&	4	&	1	&	2	&	3	&	4	&
W/S	This		song				is		Ma		kos		sa			
O/X	O		O				X		O		O		X			

HD

4/4	1	&	2	&	3	&	4	&	1	&	2	&	3	&	4	&
W/S	Play		the	beat			we		call		Ma		kos	sa		
O/X	O		X	O			X		O		X		X	X		

PR

4/4	1	&	2	&	3	&	4	&	1	&	2	&	3	&	4	&
W/S	Play			the			rhy	thm			like		this			
O/X	X			X			X	X			X		X			

Dancing Drum © 2010

Introduce PR Rhythm
LD plays Signature Rhythm
HD plays HD Rhythm - PR plays PR Rhythm

MAKOSSA
DRUM

♩ = 105 *Feel in 2*

PR Rhythm - Standard Notation

Traditional, arranged by Dancing Drum

OPTIONAL: Drum Break
All instruments play DB in unison
DB can be played at any level

CD Track: **48**

KEY	LOW	MID/HIGH
SOUND	Boom	Ba
SYMBOL	O	X

DRUM

Drum Break (DB) - Rhythm Phonics

Traditional, arranged by Dancing Drum

DB

4/4	1	&	2	&	3	&	4	&	1	&	2	&	3	&	4	&
W/S	It's		the		break		for		Ma		kos				sa	
O/X	O		O		X		X		O		O				O	

4/4	1	&	2	&	3	&	4	&	1	&	2	&	3	&	4	&
W/S	play	the		drum	break		right		now							
O/X	X	X		X	X		X		O							

Drum Break (DB) - Standard Notation

DB

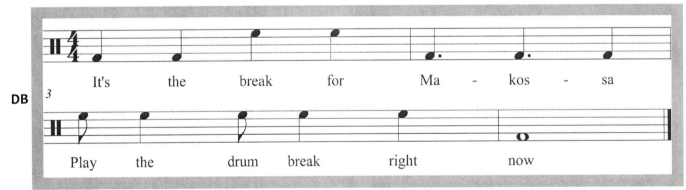

It's   the   break   for   Ma - kos - sa

Play   the   drum   break   right   now

Dancing Drum © 2010

Play Full Arrangement
DB + Level 3 + DB

CD Track: **49**

MAKOSSA
DRUM

♩ = 105 *Feel in 2*

Full Arrangement

Traditional, arranged by Dancing Drum

Dancing Drum © 2010

MAKOSSA
XYLOPHONE

LEARNING LEVELS

LEVEL 1 ★☆☆☆☆ **Introduce Signature Bass Ostinato (BX)**
BX, AX, SX play Signature Ostinato

LEVEL 2 ★★☆☆☆ **Introduce Alto Ostinato (AX)**
BX & SX play Signature Ostinato
AX plays AX Ostinato

LEVEL 3 ★★★☆☆ **Introduce Soprano Ostinato (SX)**
BX plays Signature Ostinato
AX plays AX Ostinato, SX plays SX Ostinato

LEVEL 4 ★★★★☆ **Melody 1 (M1) Arrangement**
Level 3 + M1 + downbeat ending

LEVEL 5 ★★★★★ **Full Arrangement**
Level 3 + M1 + M2 + M2 Ending

BREAK **Break Ending** **OPTIONAL: Introduce Break Ending (BE)**
All instruments play BE in unison
BE can be played at any level

Our teacher, Bioma, playing his homemade xylophone
with keys made from melted car pistons

♩ = 105 *Recommended Tempo*
Feel in 2

XYLOPHONE

NOTATION KEY
SX = Soprano Xylophone
AX = Alto Xylophone
BX = Bass Xylophone
LD = Low Drum
PR = Percussion
M1 = Melody 1
M2 = Melody 2

SUGGESTED ARRANGEMENT

> **Level 1** = 1 part ostinato
> **Level 2** = 2 part ostinato
> **Level 3** = 3 part ostinato
> **Level 4** = 3 part ostinato + M1
> **Level 5** = 3 part ostinato + M1 + M2

Levels 1-3

1. BX, PR play 8 bars, then AX plays.
2. BX, PR and AX play 8 bars, then SX plays.
3. BX, PR, AX, and SX play for 8 bars, then LD plays.
4. All instruments play ostinati for 16 bars or as many as desired.
5. Play downbeat ending.
6. Go back to measure 1 and repeat for longer arrangement.

Level 4

1. BX, PR play 8 bars, then AX plays.
2. BX, PR and AX play 8 bars, then SX plays.
3. BX, PR, AX and SX play for 8 bars, then LD plays.
4. All instruments play ostinati for 16 bars.
5. SX plays Melody 1 twice while other instruments play ostinati to 1st Ending.
6. Go back to measure 1 and repeat same arrangement to 2nd Ending.

Level 5

1. BX, PR play 8 bars, then AX plays.
2. BX, PR and AX play 8 bars, then SX plays.
3. BX, PR, AX and SX play for 8 bars, then LD plays.
4. All instruments play ostinati for 16 bars.
5. SX plays Melody 1 twice while other instruments play ostinati.
6. All instruments play ostinati for 16 bars.
7. SX plays Melody 2 four times while other instruments play ostinati to 1st Ending.
8. Go back to measure 1 and repeat same arrangement to 2nd Ending.

Break Ending *(Optional)*

1. Break Ending can be played at the end of all Level 1-5 arrangements.
2. Count 4 half notes to lead ensemble into Break Ending.
3. All instruments play Break Ending in unison.

LEVEL 1 ★☆☆☆☆

CD Track: **50**

Introduce Signature Ostinato (BX)
BX, AX, SX play Signature Ostinato

SX = Soprano Xylophone
AX = Alto Xylophone
BX = Bass Xylophone
LD = Low Drum
PR = Percussion

MAKOSSA
XYLOPHONE

♩ = 105 *Feel in 2*

Signature Ostinato (BX)

Traditional, arranged by Dancing Drum

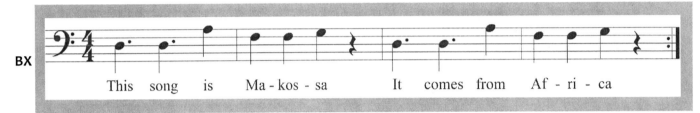

This song is Ma - kos - sa   It comes from Af - ri - ca

Introduce AX Ostinato
BX & SX play Signature Ostinato
AX plays AX Ostinato

SX = Soprano Xylophone
AX = Alto Xylophone
BX = Bass Xylophone
LD = Low Drum
PR = Percussion

CD Track: **51**

Introduce SX Ostinato
BX plays Signature Ostinato
AX plays AX Ostinato, SX plays SX Ostinato

SX = Soprano Xylophone
AX = Alto Xylophone
BX = Bass Xylophone
LD = Low Drum
PR = Percussion

LEVEL 3 ★★★☆☆

CD Track: **52**

MAKOSSA
XYLOPHONE

♩ = 105 *Feel in 2*

Soprano Ostinato (SX)

Traditional, arranged by Dancing Drum

Let's play Ma - kos - sa   It's from Bur - ki - na

Introduce Melody 1 (M1)
BX plays Signature Ostinato
AX plays AX Ostinato, SX plays M1

SX = Soprano Xylophone
AX = Alto Xylophone
BX = Bass Xylophone
M1 = Melody 1

MAKOSSA
XYLOPHONE

♩ = 105 *Feel in 2*

Melody 1 (M1)

Traditional, arranged by Dancing Drum

Dancing Drum © 2010

Melody 1 (M1) Arrangement
Level 3 + M1 + downbeat ending

SX = Soprano Xylophone
AX = Alto Xylophone
BX = Bass Xylophone
M1 = Melody 1
LD = Low Drum
PR = Percussion

MAKOSSA
XYLOPHONE

♩ = 105 *Feel in 2*

M1 Arrangement

Traditional, arranged by Dancing Drum

Dancing Drum © 2010

Introduce Melody 2 (M2) + M2 Ending
BX plays Signature Ostinato
AX plays AX Ostinato, SX plays M2

SX = Soprano Xylophone
AX = Alto Xylophone
BX = Bass Xylophone
M2 = Melody 1

MAKOSSA
XYLOPHONE

♩ = 105 *Feel in 2*

Melody 2 (M2)

Traditional, arranged by Dancing Drum

pickup notes for M2   **M2**   play 3x

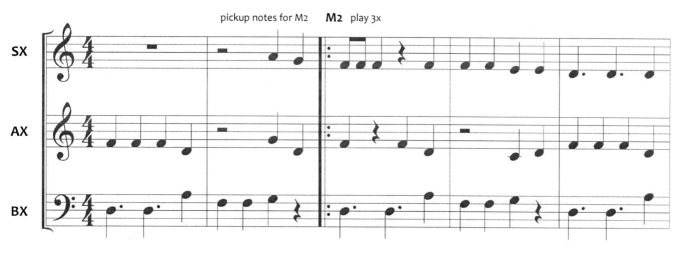

M2 Ending

Full Arrangement
Level 3 + M1 + M2 + M2 Ending

CD Track: **54**

MAKOSSA
XYLOPHONE

♩ = 105 *Feel in 2*

Full Arrangement

Traditional, arranged by Dancing Drum

Dancing Drum © 2010

MAKOSSA
XYLOPHONE

SX = Soprano Xylophone
AX = Alto Xylophone
BX = Bass Xylophone
LD = Low Drum
PR = Percussion
M1 = Melody 1
M2 = Melody 2

Dancing Drum © 2010

BREAK | **BREAK ENDING**

CD Track: 55

OPTIONAL: Introduce Break Ending (BE)
All instruments play BE in unison
BE can be played at any level

SX = Soprano Xylophone
AX = Alto Xylophone
BX = Bass Xylophone
LD = Low Drum
PR = Percussion
BE = Break Ending

MAKOSSA
XYLOPHONE

♩ = 105 *Feel in 2*

Break Ending (BE)

Traditional, arranged by Dancing Drum

It's the break for Ma - kos - sa Play the drum break right now

encountering a kids' mask parade in Bobo-Dioulasso

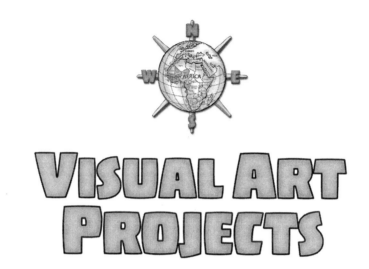

VISUAL ART PROJECTS

Art Activity
PAPER BEAD NECKLACE

SENEGAL

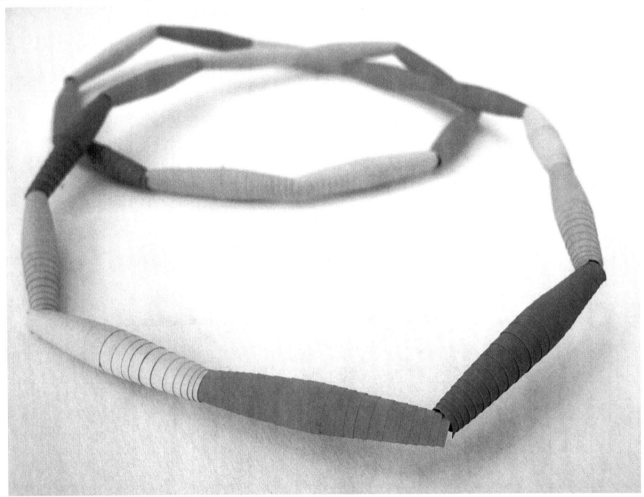

People in Africa love beads. They wear beaded necklaces, bracelets, and earrings, tie beads into their braided hair, and cover hats, bags, masks, and furniture in colorful designs made with beads. When Europeans began trading with Africa hundreds of years ago, some of the most popular items were colorful glass beads made in Italy. You can still find these "trade beads" today in Africa and throughout the world.

In addition to the *imported* beads, many different types of beads are made in West Africa. Beads are made from clay, stones, bones, metal, and *recycled* materials like glass, paper, and plastic. African-made beads come in every shape, size, and color imaginable.

Tubular beads are one of the most popular shapes. Here's an easy activity where you can make your own tube-shaped beads out of paper. Choose colorful papers and make sure that you roll enough beads for a necklace. 20 should be plenty.

MATERIALS

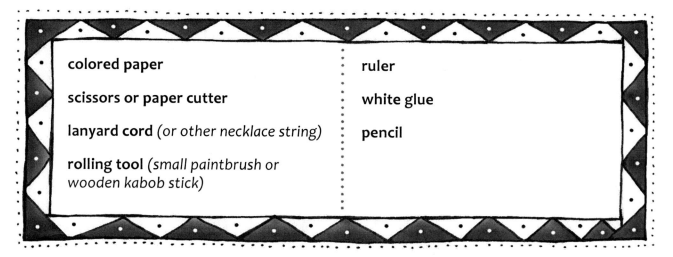

- **colored paper**
- **scissors or paper cutter**
- **lanyard cord** (or other necklace string)
- **rolling tool** (small paintbrush or wooden kabob stick)

- **ruler**
- **white glue**
- **pencil**

Estimated time for completion: **50 minutes**

STEP 1: MEASURE & CUT THE PAPER FOR YOUR BEADS

Place your paper on a flat surface. Use a ruler to measure 1½ inch sections, on the long side of your paper, lightly marking each 1½ inch with your pencil. Do the same thing along the opposite side of the paper, shifting your first mark ¾ inch away from the edge. Then use your ruler to connect the dots with light, straight lines, like the illustration below. You should have a bunch of long, skinny triangles. Use your scissors to cut out the strips of paper, and discard the partial triangle on either end. (Teachers may wish to complete this step before class with a paper cutter, or draw one template and photocopy it onto colored paper for each student to cut out.)

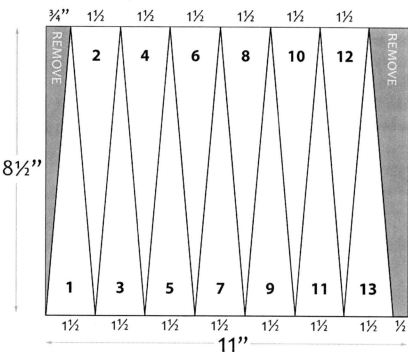

STEP 2: ROLL A BEAD

Take one triangle and lay it flat on a table, with the marked side facing up. Place your rolling tool across the wide end of the paper, and begin rolling the paper tightly around the stick. It may take a few tries to learn how to roll the bead symmetrically. Roll the paper all the way to the point of the triangle.

STEP 3: GLUE THE BEAD

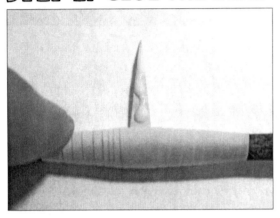

Place a small dab of glue on the end point and roll it up until your bead is complete. Hold the glued end in place for a few moments until it sticks. Carefully slide your bead off the rolling tool, put the bead on a string to dry, and start another bead.

STEP 4: MAKE YOUR NECKLACE

Cut a length of string for your finished necklace, making sure the string is at least long enough to fit over your head. Thread your beads on the string. You can add other beads from the store if you want to. When your string is full, tie the ends together with a square knot. Trim the extra string and tuck the ends into the beads.

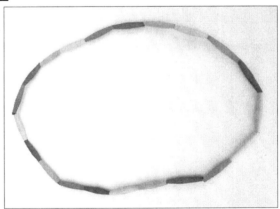

STEP 5: OPTIONAL

You can paint your finished beads with tempera or acrylic paint. Make African-style, geometric patterns of dots and lines.

Art Activity
DJEMBEFOLA HAT

STANDARDS:
NA-VA.K-4.1, 4, 6
NA-VA.5-8.3, 4, 5, 6
NL-ENG.K-12.3, 9

GUINEA

A *djembefola* is a master *djembe* player. When performing, a djembefola sometimes wears a special, colorful hat. A traditional djembefola hat is made of handwoven fabrics, beads, *cowrie shells*, mirrors, and fur that looks like a horse's mane or the mane of a lion. The spectacular hat makes the djembefola look as impressive as he or she sounds!

Here are some instructions for how to make your own djembefola hat from common materials in your classroom, like poster board, staples, paint, and glue. If you prefer to make your hat from fabric, this activity can be easily adapted to use colorful felt cloth. It's simple to sew with a needle and thread.

MATERIALS

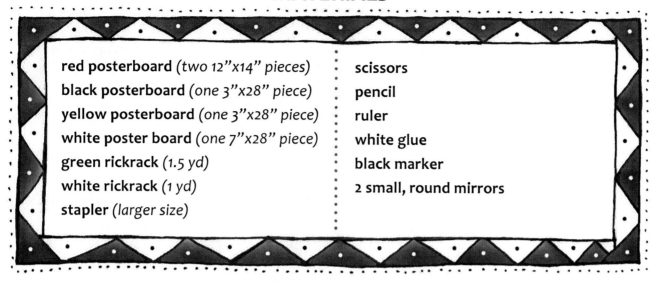

red posterboard *(two 12"x14" pieces)*

black posterboard *(one 3"x28" piece)*

yellow posterboard *(one 3"x28" piece)*

white poster board *(one 7"x28" piece)*

green rickrack *(1.5 yd)*

white rickrack *(1 yd)*

stapler *(larger size)*

scissors

pencil

ruler

white glue

black marker

2 small, round mirrors

Estimated time for completion: **90 minutes**

STEP 1: DRAW & CUT HAT PARTS FROM POSTERBOARD

1) <u>2 RED HAT PANELS</u> – Take one piece of red poster board, a pencil and a ruler, and make a light mark in the center of the 12" side, on top and bottom. On the 14" sides, make marks at 4" and 9" from the bottom corners. Draw arcs connecting the 9" marks with the 6" mark at the top. The two arcs should meet at a point. Draw arcs connecting the 4" marks with the 6" mark at the bottom, leaving a space of about ¾" between the arcs at the bottom. Your shape should look like the pattern to the right. Cut out the first Red Hat Panel and use it to trace and cut the second Red Hat Panel, so the two pieces are exactly the same.

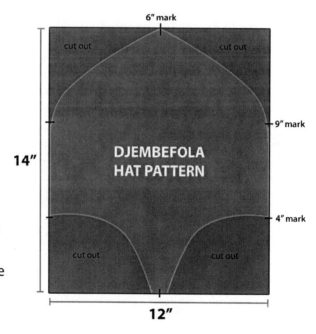

2) <u>YELLOW HEADBAND</u> – This fits snugly around your head and will be attached to the *inside* of the hat. Cut a strip of yellow poster board 3" wide and 28" long. Wrap the strip around your head, just above the ears. Hold it so that the headband is sized to fit snugly, remove from your head, and staple twice where the paper overlaps. You can trim the excess paper off now. Set aside.

3) <u>BLACK HATBAND</u> – This fits around the *outside* of your hat. Cut a strip of black poster board 3" wide and 28" long. Set aside.

STEP 1: DRAW & CUT HAT PARTS FROM POSTERBOARD *(cont.)*

4) <u>WHITE FRINGE PIECES</u> – These go along the *top* of your hat. Cut a long strip of white poster board that's 7" wide and 28" long. Using the edge of a ruler and the pointy end of a paintbrush, score down the length of the strip and fold the strip in half. Cut into 10-12 pieces of folded paper, measuring about 2.5"x7", like the illustration below shows.

28"

cut											3.5"
score	& fold										
cut											3.5"

7"

2.5"

STEP 2: ATTACH WHITE FRINGE TO 1st RED HAT PANEL

Select one Red Hat Panel and staple the White Fringe Pieces to the inside edge, beginning 2" above the corner. Work your way around the top and down the other side, overlapping and stapling each White Fringe Piece once. Make sure to stop 2" above the 4" mark on both sides.

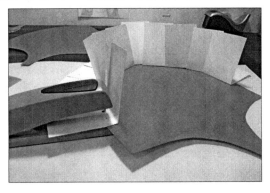

STEP 3: ATTACH 2nd RED HAT PANEL

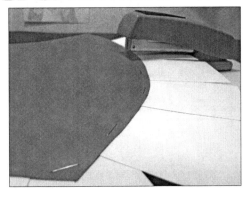

Place the second Red Hat Panel on top of the first. The panels should line up very closely, and the white fringe should be sandwiched in between the red panels. Use your stapler to tack the edges together, starting where the white fringe begins, 2" above the 4" mark. Do not staple the last 2" on either side.

STEP 4: CUT THE WHITE FRINGE

Use a pair of scissors to "fringe" the white poster board by making even, vertical cuts through each section, about 1/8" wide. Separate the fringes with your fingers.

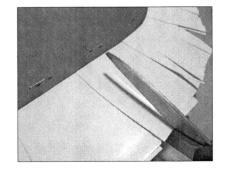

GUINEA

STEP 5: ATTACH BLACK HATBAND

Overlap the ends of the black strip of poster board to make a circle that fits around the outside of your hat, just beneath the White Fringe. Staple in place over earflaps, once or twice on each side.

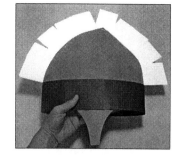

STEP 6: ATTACH YELLOW HEADBAND

Slip the yellow headband inside the hat and staple once on each earflap. Test your hat to make sure it fits correctly.

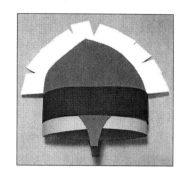

STEP 7: DECORATE YOUR HAT!

1) **GREEN RICKRACK** – Use white glue to attach green rickrack around the edges of the red panels, covering staples with the trim. Tuck the ends under the black hatband.

2) **WHITE RICKRACK** – Cut two 12" pieces of white rickrack. Tuck the end into the black hatband, and glue along the center of the earflap, so several inches dangle off the edge. Cut 2 extra pieces of white rickrack, 8" long. Fold in half and staple to the dangling trim. Cut a small piece of yellow poster board, fold around and glue it over the staple.

3) **FINISHING TOUCHES** – You can finish your hat with paint, beads, and other materials however you like. For this design, we created "cowrie shells" out of white poster board, cutting an almond shape and drawing a black zig-zag down the middle with a marker. We glued 4 shells to each side of the mask, and finished the design by gluing a 1" round mirror in the center of the shells. You can also use paint to make colorful designs on the hat. Have fun and be creative when finishing your Djembefola Hat!

STANDARDS:
NA-VA.K-4.1, 2, 4, 6
NA-VA.5-8.3, 4, 5, 6
NA-D.5-8.3
NL-ENG.K-12.3, 9

Art Activity
DOGON KANAGA MASK

MALI

The *Dogon* people of Mali are known for their fine masks. One of their most important masks is the *Kanaga*. To the Dogon, Kanaga represents the universe. Carved from wood, the mask has a central mast and two sets of legs. The headpiece of the mask points both up and down, recognizing the sky overhead *(the world of the ancestors)*, and the earth beneath our feet *(the world of the living)*.

The dance of the Kanaga mask includes powerful jumps and sweeping, round motions that touch the top of the mask to the earth. In addition to the mask, the dancer wears a skirt of red and black plant fibers and a vest covered in *cowrie shells*. Kanaga dancers appear in large groups of 20 or more at a time, creating an impressive scene for the audience.

The Kanaga mask is *traditionally* painted in colors of black, white, and burnt sienna or red. These colors occur in the natural environment of the Dogon, who create pigments from colorful soils, minerals, and plants.

Here are instructions for making your own Kanaga Mask from poster board and paint.

MATERIALS

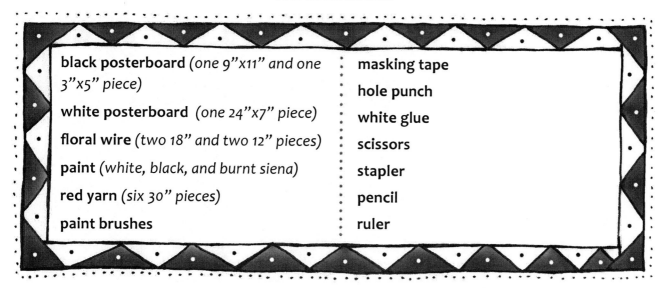

black posterboard *(one 9"x11" and one 3"x5" piece)*

white posterboard *(one 24"x7" piece)*

floral wire *(two 18" and two 12" pieces)*

paint *(white, black, and burnt siena)*

red yarn *(six 30" pieces)*

paint brushes

masking tape

hole punch

white glue

scissors

stapler

pencil

ruler

Estimated time for completion: **90 minutes**

STEP 1: DRAW & CUT THE 4 PARTS FROM POSTER BOARD

1) <u>**FACE MASK**</u> – Use a ruler and pencil to draw the pattern to the right on a 9"x11" piece of black poster board. With scissors, cut the Face Mask out around the lines. Remove eyeholes. Cut a 3" slit in the middle of the top, overlap edges and staple twice to give the mask form. Set aside and make the headpiece.

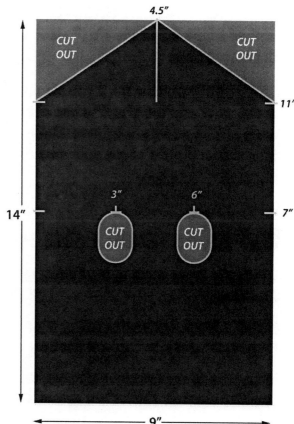

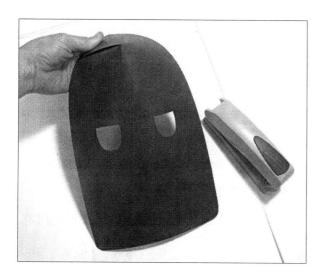

2) **HEADPIECE** - Using your 24"x7" piece of white poster board, a pencil and a ruler, and a pair of scissors, mark and cut the following shapes:

    a) **Center Mast** – 3"x16" *(Use masking tape to attach two 18" floral wires to the back for support. Make sure the wire extends from the bottom edge by 4", and bend the extra wire at a 30° angle.)*

    b) **2 Cross Arms** - 2"x16" each *(tape one 12" floral wire up the back of each for support)*

    c) **4 Small Rectangles** - 2"x5" each

	16"		2"	2"	2"	2"
3"	*Center Mast*	3"x16"	2x5"	2x5"	2x5"	2x5"
2"	*Cross Arm*	2"x16"				
2"	*Cross Arm*	2"x16"	CUT OUT			

7"

24"

The pieces of your headpiece should look like the image above, with wires taped to the 3 longest pieces.

3) **DIAMOND SHAPE CONNECTOR** – Cut a diamond shape out of the 3"x5" piece of black poster board.

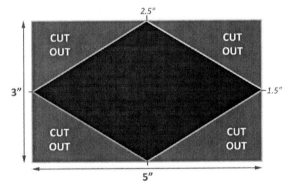

2.5"

CUT OUT   CUT OUT

3"   1.5"

CUT OUT   CUT OUT

5"

4) **HEADBAND** *(optional)* – if you plan to wear the mask, use the 2"x28" piece of black poster board to make a headband. Make a headband that fits just above your ears and staple to size. Set aside.

STEP 2: ASSEMBLE THE HEADPIECE

1) **Attach the Cross Arms to the Center Mast** with white glue, leaving a 4" space at the top and bottom.

2) **Attach 4 Small Rectangles to the ends of the Cross Arms** with white glue. Make sure the top rectangles point up and the bottom rectangles point down.

3) Allow glue to dry for a few minutes, then **punch holes where the Cross Arms and Small Rectangles overlap**, 4 holes in a square shape for each overlapping point.

MALI

STEP 3: ATTACH THE MASK & HEADPIECE

Once you have the Face Mask and Headpiece made, it's time to put them together.

1) <u>Insert the wires</u> of the Center Mast into the pocket at the top of the Face Mask.

2) <u>Place the Diamond Shape Connector</u> over the joint and staple in at least 4 spots to attach securely to the top and bottom of the mask.

3) <u>Lay the mask face-down</u> and drip a few drops of white glue into the joint where the top and bottom meet. Allow to dry.

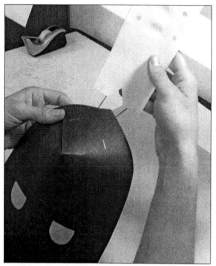

Slide the headpiece wires into the pocket at the top of the Face Mask.

Break and return in hour 2 for the next steps

STEP 4: DECORATE THE MASK

1) <u>Paint the corners</u> and overlapping spots of the Headpiece black.

2) <u>Paint the Face Mask</u> with white and burnt sienna paints, being careful not to crush the paper form.

3) When paint is dry, <u>weave red yarn</u> through hole punches in a boxed "X" pattern. Tie with a knot in the back and trim extra yarn.

Weave red yarn through hole punches

STEP 5: FINISH THE MASK

If you plan to display the mask on a wall, your project is already finished. If you would like to wear the mask, now is the time to attach the headband to the inside of the mask. Staple the headband to the inside edges of the mask, and test to see if it fits correctly. Make sure you can see through the eyeholes.

STANDARDS:
NA-VA.K-4.1, 2, 3, 4, 5, 6
NA-VA.5-8.3, 4, 5, 6
NSS-G.K-12.4
NL-ENG.K-12.3, 9

Art Activity

WOODABE POUCH

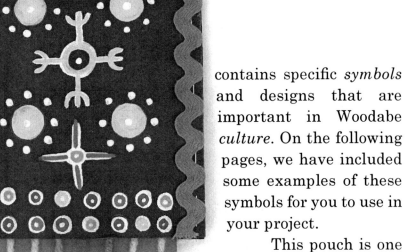

NIGER

The *Woodabe* are one of Africa's most interesting and colorful *ethnic groups*. A branch of the *Fulani* family, Woodabes are *nomads* who travel long distances through West Africa to take their herds of cows, goats, and sheep to green pastures. Woodabes consider themselves to be the most beautiful people in the world, and they spend extraordinary amounts of time, energy, and money adorning themselves with beautiful make up, clothes, and jewelry.

Every item that a Woodabe person uses to decorate him or herself contains specific *symbols* and designs that are important in Woodabe *culture*. On the following pages, we have included some examples of these symbols for you to use in your project.

This pouch is one example of an everyday item (a wallet) that Woodabe people have turned into a work of art so beautiful that it's worn as jewelery. Though these kinds of pouches are usually made of fabric or leather covered with colorful designs, this project uses materials commonly found in classrooms, like poster board, paint, and yarn.

MATERIALS

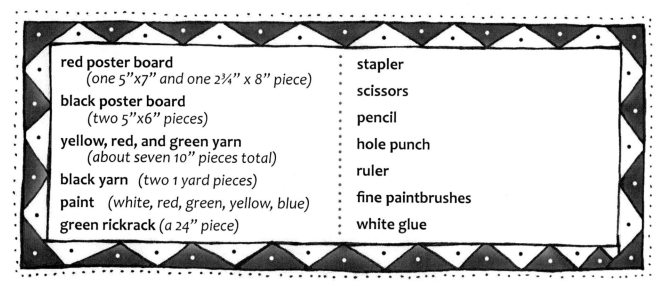

red poster board
(one 5"x7" and one 2¾" x 8" piece)

black poster board
(two 5"x6" pieces)

yellow, red, and green yarn
(about seven 10" pieces total)

black yarn *(two 1 yard pieces)*

paint *(white, red, green, yellow, blue)*

green rickrack *(a 24" piece)*

stapler

scissors

pencil

hole punch

ruler

fine paintbrushes

white glue

Estimated time for completion: **90 minutes**

STEP 1: MEASURE & CUT THE PARTS OF YOUR POUCH

1) RED INNER POUCH – Cut a 5" x 7" piece of red poster board. Following the diagram below, score on the dotted lines by placing a ruler along the line and firmly running the pointy end of a paintbrush along it. This will press a line into the paper that will help you to fold it more easily. With a pair of scissors, cut small slits into each score, ¼" down from the top edge and 1" up from the bottom edge. Fold along the scores, overlap the flaps, and staple them in place with 2-3 staples, making the sleeve of your pouch.

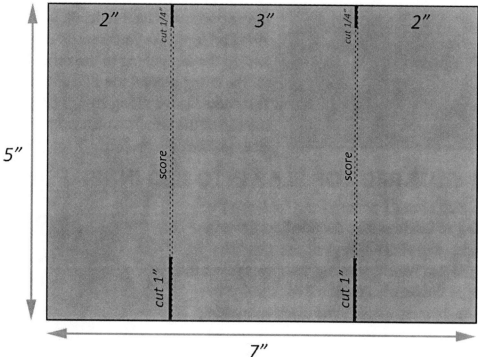

STEP 1: MEASURE & CUT THE PARTS OF POUCH (cont.)

2) **RED TOP FLAP** - Cut an 8" x 2.75" piece of red poster board. Following the diagram to the right, make a score through the middle with the pointy end of a paintbrush. You can cut the outside edge with an arc or diagonal lines meeting in a point.

3) **BLACK OUTER POUCH** – Start with 2 pieces of black poster board that measure 5" x 6". Following the pattern to the right, measure and cut one piece out, and then trace it to make the second one. You'll need 2 finished pieces that are exactly the same. Set both pieces aside.

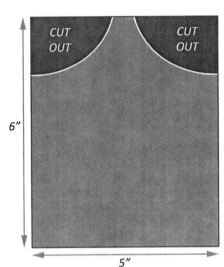

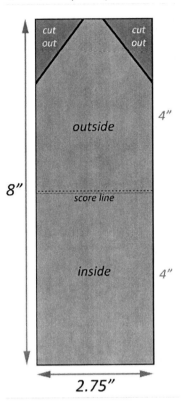

STEP 2: CUT & ATTACH NECK STRAP

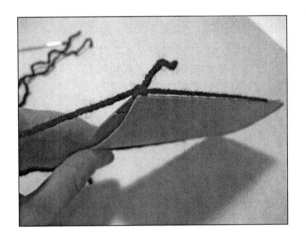

Cut 2 pieces of black yarn, 1 yard each. Run one piece through the inside of the Red Inner Pouch, setting the string into the side slits so it stays in place. Loop the string around the side of the pouch and tie it to itself, leaving a long string on top. Take your second piece of yarn and do the same thing to the other side, tying off the string around the side of the pouch. This should leave 2 long strings coming from the top of the pouch, which will be tied off later to finish the project.

STEP 3: GLUE RED TOP FLAP INTO RED INNER POUCH

Your Red Top Flap should be scored and folded in the middle, making an inside and an outside flap. Cover one side of the inside flap with white glue, and carefully insert it into the Red Pouch, pressing the glue against the stapled inside of the pouch. Fold the Red Top Flap over the front of the Red Inner Pouch and place something heavy on top of it for a few minutes to help it dry flat.

STEP 4: ASSEMBLE BLACK OUTER POUCH

Stack your two black pieces on top of each other so all of the edges meet up. Measure ¼" in from the sides, make a light line, and staple along the line 5-6 times. Make another line of 2-3 staples 2" from the top, making sure to leave space at the corners for the string to pass through. Do not staple the bottom edge.

STEP 5: DECORATE BLACK OUTER POUCH

Glue rickrack over the staples, front and back. Choose some Woodabe Decorative Symbols from the drawings below for the front of your pouch. Draw the designs in pencil first, and then use a fine paintbrush to fill them in. Since you're painting on black paper, you should paint your designs with white first, and then do a layer of colored paint on top of the white when it's dry. Use red, green, yellow, and blue colors, like the Woodabe do.

WOODABE DECORATIVE SYMBOLS

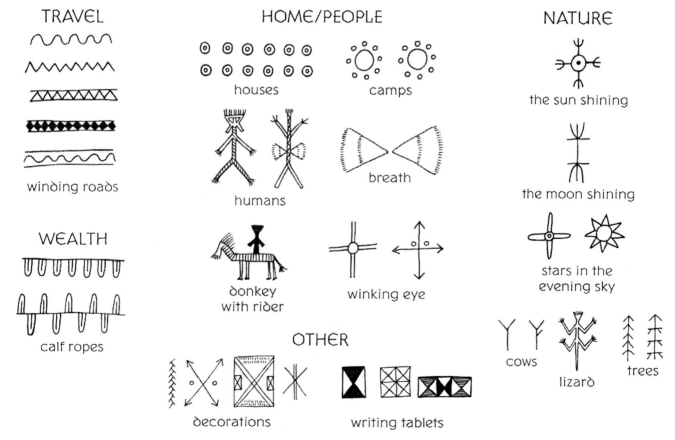

TRAVEL

winding roads

WEALTH

calf ropes

HOME/PEOPLE

houses

camps

humans

breath

donkey with rider

winking eye

OTHER

decorations

writing tablets

NATURE

the sun shining

the moon shining

stars in the evening sky

cows

lizard

trees

STEP 6: DECORATE RED INNER POUCH

Using a hole punch, make 5-7 holes along the bottom of your red pouch, at least ½" from the edge. Cut 10" pieces of red, yellow, and green yarn and tie through holes to make a fringe. Trim the fringe to make it even. If you have time, you can use some of the Woodabe Decorative Symbols to decorate the Top Flap of your Inner Pouch. Draw the designs in pencil first and finish with a fine black or brown marker.

STEP 7: FINISH YOUR POUCH

When the paint is dry on the Black Outer Pouch, it's time to insert the Inner Pouch. Thread the long ends of the black yarn through the inside of the Outer Pouch, and push them out through the top corners with the pointy tip of a paintbrush. Do the same thing for both strings, and pull them through until the Red Inner Pouch nests completely inside the Black Outer Pouch. The Inner Pouch should slide easily in and out of the Outer Pouch. Tie the ends of the strings so that you can wear the pouch as a long necklace.

A Woodabe Man
with his beautiful face paint, turban, hat, jewelery, and clothing

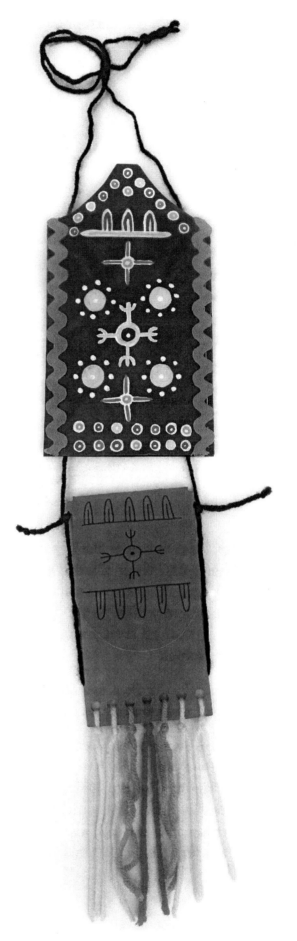

STANDARDS:
NA-VA.K-4.1, 2, 4, 6
NA-VA.5-8.3, 4, 5, 6
NA-D.5-8.3
NL-ENG.K-12.3, 9

Art Activity
Bwa Hawk Mask

BURKINA FASO

The *Hawk Mask* is one of the key characters in the *Bwa masquerade*. This mask is carved from a flat plank of wood and covered in painted designs in colors of white, black, and red. Target-shaped eyes and a round mouth are surrounded by triangles and zigzag lines in black and white. To the Bwa, this pattern signifies the "path of the *ancestors*," a way of living that all Bwa must follow to succeed in life. The Hawk Mask is topped with a red beak shape.

With this mask, the Bwa are not attempting to create an exact copy of a real hawk. Instead, they are creating an *abstract* version with qualities important to Bwa society.

The hawk represents the Bwa connection to the natural world. By dancing the hawk mask, the Bwa honor the hawk's hunting skills, an action that they believe will bring blessings from the hawk during the hunt. The dancer wearing the mask mimics the motion of a hawk in flight, quickly diving to either side and spinning the mask right and left around his head. This *vigorous* dance is made more impressive by an enormous costume of plant fibers that swirls around the dancer with each move.

MATERIALS

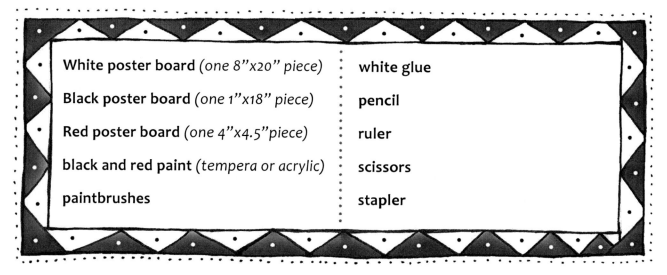

White poster board *(one 8"x20" piece)*

Black poster board *(one 1"x18" piece)*

Red poster board *(one 4"x4.5"piece)*

black and red paint *(tempera or acrylic)*

paintbrushes

white glue

pencil

ruler

scissors

stapler

Estimated time for completion: **60 minutes**

STEP I: MEASURE & CUT THE PIECES OF YOUR MASK

a) WHITE PLANK MASK – Using an 8" x 20" piece of white poster board, a pencil, and a ruler, draw 2 arcs under the wings of the mask, and a long, shallow "U" on top of the mask. Following the illustration below, draw triangles for eyeholes and a circular mouth. Cut out the outline of your mask, and remove the mouth and eyes. Cut a 2" slit into the middle of the top of the mask.

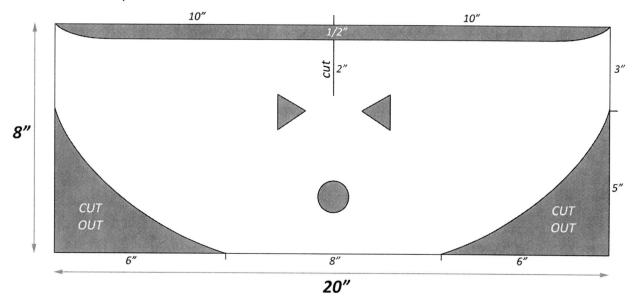

b) BLACK TRIANGLES – Cut a long strip of black poster board 1" thick and 18" long. Use a pair of scissors to cut a zigzag of triangles across the paper. Set aside.

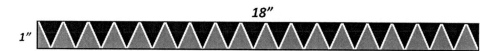

STEP 1: MEASURE & CUT THE PIECES OF YOUR MASK (cont.)

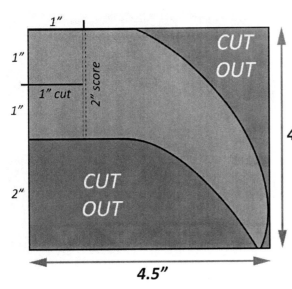

1"
1"
1" cut
2" score
1"
2"
CUT OUT
CUT OUT
4"
4.5"

BURKINA FASO

c) **RED BEAK** – Using a 4" x 4.5" piece of red poster board, measure 2" down on the 4" side and make a mark. This will be the starting point for the bottom of the Red Beak shape. Following the design to the left, make 2 arcs that meet in a point for the shape of the beak. Make a tab for attaching the beak by measuring a 1" x 2" box on the upper edge of the beak. Cut a slit 1" deep through the middle. With the pointy edge of a paintbrush, score a mark 1" from the left edge. The score will make folding the paper easier. Set Red Beak aside.

STEP 2: PAINT HAWK EYES & MOUTH

The hawk eyes are painted in a target pattern, like the design to the right. Start with the inner black circle and paint 3 concentric black circles around the center, leaving white space between each ring. Fill in the middle ring with red paint. The Hawk Eyes should not measure more than 3" around at the widest point.

Paint around the mouth with one red circle, and outline the red circle with black.

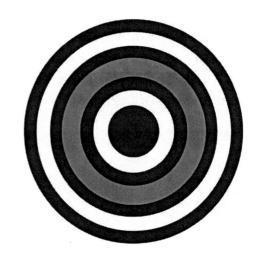

STEP 3: PLACE & GLUE BLACK TRIANGLES

Lay your triangles in a design on the surface of the mask before attaching with glue. Make a diagonal line from the bottom of the mask to the top, assembling the triangles so they touch at the corners. Lay a row of triangles across the top. Do the same pattern on both sides, making sure your mask is symmetrical. When you're happy with the design, glue the triangles to the mask, one by one.

STEP 4: COMPLETE DESIGN WITH BLACK PAINT

Paint a black line near the edge of your line of triangles. Decorate the interior of the mask with geometric black shapes. Make sure to leave the outer wing area of the mask white.

STEP 5: ATTACH RED BEAK

Glue Red Beak tabs to back of mask.

Bend the tabs of your Red Beak along the score line, one to the left and the other to the right. Insert the beak into the slit at the top of your mask, and glue the tabs to the back side of the mask. Hold in place for a few moments to dry.

STEP 6: FINISH THE MASK

If the wings of the mask are too floppy, take an 18" piece of floral wire and tape it across the back of your mask with masking tape. If you would like to wear the mask, make a headband from a strip of black poster board, stapled in a circle to fit just above your ears. Staple the headband to the back of the mask with 2-3 staples.

woman carrying water with her "I Love Africa" bucket

ADDITIONAL RESOURCES

GLOSSARY

abstract - in art, using shapes, colors, and lines in a unique way to create an image of a subject, without attempting to make an exact representation

acacia - a resilient type of tree that grows in the desert and Sahel areas of West Africa

accenting - placing a strong emphasis on a musical note or on a syllable of a word

accompaniment - a musical part played together with and in support of other parts

adapted - changed to survive in a new climate or culture

Afropop - a style of African music that combines traditional and modern music

ancestor - family member who lived before our time, sometimes hundreds of years ago

anthropologist - a scientist that studies human origins, cultures, social customs, and beliefs

Arabic - of or relating to the Arab world in North Africa and the Middle East. A language.

arid - extremely dry, without rainfall or moisture

bala, or **balafon** - West African xylophone

ballet - the French word for "dance"

Bambara - a Mande ethnic group, the largest in Mali

baobab - a unique type of tree that grows in the West African Sahel, sometimes called the "upside down tree" because its limbs look like roots.

Bobo - an ethnic group of Burkina Faso. Also the short name for Burkina's 2nd largest city, Bobo-Dioulasso.

boubou - a type of long, flowing robe, often brightly colored and embroidered, worn by men and women in West Africa

breakthrough - a significant achievement or sudden advance in status

Burkinabé - a person from Burkina Faso

bush pig - a wild hog that lives in the forests and savannas of West Africa

bush taxi - a type of shared public transport in West Africa, usually a van, that travels long distances through remote areas

Bwa - an ethnic group of Burkina Faso known for their beautiful masks

calabash - a type of spherical gourd that grows on a vine. Calabashes can be used for many purposes, including carrying things and for percussion instruments.

caravan - a group of travelers journeying together on camels

CFA - the symbol for the West African franc. One US dollar is equal to about 515 CFA.

chief - the highest ranking leader of a village or city

choreographer - a person who composes the movements of a dance

chorus - a phrase of music played or sung by several people at once

climate - the general weather conditions of a region

conservation - the supervision of natural resources to preserve and protect them

contiguous - touching or bordering

cowrie shells - a type of small, white sea shell used for early African money, adornment, and fortune-telling

crescendo - a gradual increase in volume

crescent - the curving shape of the moon in its first or last quarter

cultivating - working the land to raise crops

culture - the shared customs, traditions, and language of a group of people through the course of history

debuted - showed or performed for the first time

desertification - the process of desert overtaking other lands

desolate - solitary, lonely, far away, like an empty landscape without trees or water

diversity - variety, different types of people, and different ways of life coexisting in a community

djeli - the traditional musician history-keepers of West Africa, from the Mande line. Also called "griot".

djembe - a type of West African drum shaped like a goblet, skinned with a goat hide, and played with the hands

djembefola - a master of the djembe drum

djun-djun - a type of West African drum shaped like a cylinder, skinned with cow hide, and played with sticks. Also called dundun or doon.

Dogon - an ancient ethnic group that lives in the area of the Bandiagara cliffs in central Mali, known for their interesting masks and culture

doundoun - a type of cylindrical bass drum, played with a curved stick, from Niger

drum break - a rhythmic phrase played to unify the drum ensemble at intervals throughout a performance piece

dundun - a type of West African drum shaped like a cylinder, skinned with cow hide, and played with straight sticks. Also called djun-djun or doon.

dundunba - the largest and lowest pitched drum in the dundun family

eerie - mysterious and weird

ensemble - a group of musicians playing together

ethnic group - a group of people sharing a distinct language, history, culture, and general geographic area

folk song - a song which has been handed down from generation to generation by oral tradition

foreigner - a person from another country

Fouta Djallon - a picturesque mountain chain in Guinea, homeland of the Fulani people

Fulani - an ethnic group found throughout West Africa. Fulanis are traditionally nomadic herders.

Fulfulde - a general name for the language spoken by Fulanis

gasu - a Nigerien name for a calabash

geometric - with angles, lines, and well-defined shapes

gita - a type of shaker made from a calabash with cowrie shells or beads tied to the rim

goje - a Nigerien name for a monochord violin

gourd - a hard-shelled fruit that grows from a type of vine. Gourds are harvested, dried, and used for many purposes in West Africa, including musical instruments

griot - the traditional musician history-keepers of West Africa, from the Mande line. Also called "djeli".

Guinean - someone or something from Guinea

Hausa - an ethnic group living mostly in Niger and Nigeria

harvest - the gathering of ripened crops

homeland - place of home or origin

homo sapiens - the scientific name (genus and species) for modern humans

hyena - a dog-like, wild carnivore that lives in the savannas of Africa

imported - something that is brought from a foreign country

indigo - a dark blue dye obtained from a type of plant that grows in West Africa

initiation - a ceremony that marks the transition from childhood to adulthood

integrity - honesty; soundness of moral character

irrigation - watering of crops to assist in their growth

international - involving two or more nations or their citizens

Jola - an ethnic group and language common in southern Senegal, The Gambia, and Guinea Bissau.

Jula - a Mande ethnic group and language common in Burkina Faso and Côte D'Ivoire. Also spelled "Dioula".

kakaki - a long, narrow trumpet with one note, played by the Hausa people in Niger and Nigeria

kalangou - the Hausa name for a talking drum

kamele n'goni - a type of harp from Mali made from a calabash, a long stick, and fishing line, literally, "the young man's harp"

kariyan - a percussion instrument made from a tube of iron, scored crosswise. A thin piece of metal is rubbed across the score marks to make a scraping sound.

kenkeni - the smallest and highest pitched drum of the dundun family

konkoni - a dundun-like drum made from a metal can and goat or cow hide, played with a wooden stick with a perpendicular tip and a small bell

kora - a West African harp played by djelis, made of a large calabash, a curved stick, and 21 strings

ksing-ksing - a type of metal rattle inserted into the ropes of a djembe drum

landlocked - without direct access to the sea or ocean, surrounded on all sides by land

livestock - animals like cows, goats, sheep, horses, and poultry that are kept and raised for human purposes including food and transportation

lyrics - the words to a song

M

Malian - someone or something from Mali

Malinké - a Mande ethnic group and language common in Mali, Guinea, Senegal and other countries in West Africa

mallet - a stick with a bulbous end, used to play percussion instruments like balafons and drums

Mande - a name that refers to cultures, ethnic groups, and languages in West Africa that are descended from the powerful Mande, or Mali, Empire of the 13th century

marimba - a descendant of West African balafons consisting of graduated wooden slats and resonators attached to a frame, played in orchestras around the world and especially in Latin America.

masquerade - a gathering where the performers or attendees wear masks

mbalax - a style of popular music from Senegal, based on the rhythms of sabar drumming

megaphone - a hand-held, cone-shaped device for amplifying the voice

merchant - a person who sells things at a market or store; a trader

melody - a musical phrase, or rhythmical pattern of notes, in a composition

millet - a type of nutritious grain commonly grown in the West African Sahel

mimic - imitate or copy in action or speech

mollo - the Songhai or Zarma name for a 3-stringed lute, ancestor to the American banjo

monochord - having a single string

Mòoré - the language spoken by the Mossi people in Burkina Faso

mortar and pestle - a food grinding tool consisting of a bowl and a stick. The stick is used to pound or grind the contents of the bowl (grains, spices, etcetera) into a fine consistency.

mosque - a Muslim place of worship

Mossi - the most numerous ethnic group in Burkina Faso

Nigerien - someone or something from Niger

nomadic - the descriptive term for a person or ethnic group that moves from place to place, in search of pasture for livestock, food, or trading opportunities, without a permanent home

oasis - a small, green area with water resources in a desert region

passport - identification document issued by a country of citizenship which allows the holder to cross borders and travel between different countries

percussionist - a musician who plays percussion instruments

pirogue - a type of flat-bottomed, canoe-shaped boat common throughout Africa, used mainly for river travel

plateau - a flat, high land area usually cut by deep canyons and bounded by cliffs

polyrhythm - a style of music using more than one rhythm played at the same time

Pular - the language spoken by the Fulani people in Guinea

quartet - a musical ensemble with four members

recycled - something that has been used once and then re-worked for another use

rehearsal - practice for the purpose of improvement, often in preparation for a public show

remote - far away from cities or towns; secluded

research - careful investigation into a subject to discover facts or revise theories

resonance - the volume, vibration, and sound quality of an instrument

rhythm - a pattern of notes or beats in time

sabar - a style of drum and drumming from Senegal, performed mainly by the Wolof people

Sahara - the world's largest desert, from the Arabic word for "desert"

Sahel - a geographic climate zone on the southern edge, or shore, of the Sahara Desert, stretching from Senegal to Chad. From the Arabic word for "shore"

safari - a travel adventure or expedition, from the Swahili word for "journey"

sangban - the middle-sized and mid-pitched drum in the dundun family

savanna - a flat grassland with scattered trees and seasonal rains

sedentary - living in one place; not nomadic

Senegalese - someone or something from Senegal

solo - a leading performance by one musician, singer, or dancer, with or without accompaniment

soloist - a person who performs a solo

Songhai - an ethnic group and language common in Mali and Niger, inhabiting a region of the Niger River from approximately Timbuktu to Niamey

strings - a family of musical instruments characterized by tightly stretched chord or wire that produces a tone when plucked or played with a bow

Sudan - a geographic climate zone south of the Sahel that shares attributes of the arid Sahel climate and the greener tropical areas to the south. Also the name of a country in eastern Africa

sugar cane - a type of plant with a stout, jointed stalk, cultivated in the tropics to produce sugar

Susu - a Mande ethnic group and language common in Guinea

Sultan - a traditional position of power in Islamic societies, functioning like a regional king

swing feel - notes or beats that are played to create a galloping or shuffling feel

symmetrical - the same on both sides

talking drum - a type of drum that can be squeezed on the sides to bring the pitch up and down to imitate a voice

tenere - the Tuareg name for the Sahara Desert

Tifinagh - the written language of the Tuareg people

toubab - the word used to refer to a foreign person in Mali and Burkina Faso

trade - the act of buying, selling, and/or exchanging goods

tradition - custom, belief, habit, or story that has been handed down from generation to generation

tropical - a very hot and humid climate, sometimes referring to the geographic location between the tropic lines near the equator

tuned - adjusted so the pitch of an instrument is in harmony

turban - a headdress consisting of a long cloth wound around the head

Tuareg - a traditionally nomadic ethnic group living mostly in Niger and Mali. Sometimes called the "Blue Men of the Sahara" because their indigo turbans dye their skin blue

unique - original, distinct; the only one of its kind

unison - all together, with one sound or voice

vigorous - strong, energetic, forceful

Wassoulou - a distinct area in southern Mali, in the Wassoulou River valley, inhabited by a mix of Bambara and Fulani people

Wolof - the largest ethnic group and most common language in Senegal

Woodabe - a nomadic ethnic group living primarily in Niger. Woodabes are a branch of the Fulani family.

xylophone - a percussion instrument consisting of a series of graduated, tuned wooden slats, played with mallets

Yassa - a style of sauce made in Senegal that mixes elements of African and French cooking

Zarma - an ethnic group and language common in Niger

Reading Comprehension Key

....

Journal Entry #1
Over the Atlantic: The Rhythm Hunters

1) Fill in the blank: Africa has over **50** countries.

2) Name the 5 regions of Africa.
West Africa, North Africa, East Africa, Central Africa, Southern Africa

3) Name 5 countries in West Africa.
Possible answers: **Senegal, Guinea, Mali, Niger, Burkina Faso, Benin, Côte D'Ivoire, Gambia, Ghana, Guinea-Bissau, Liberia, Mauritania, Nigeria, Sierra Leone, Togo**

4) Why is Africa sometimes called "The Motherland"?
Africa is where our earliest ancestors walked the earth, and it's likely where we discovered and first developed our ability to make music.

5) *Fill in the blank:* In Africa, drums are used to play music and to **communicate**.

....

Fact Sheet
How Big is Africa?

1) How does the size of your country compare to the region of West Africa?
Possible answer for the 48 contiguous US states: **The lower 48 states of the USA have an area of 3.12 million mi^2. The surface area of West Africa is approximately 3.11 million mi^2. These two areas are basically equal in size.** (Students may wish to calculate the comparison using the entire area of the 50 US states.)

2) How does the size of your country compare to West Africa's largest country, Niger?
Possible answers for the 48 contiguous US states: **Niger has a land area of 489,000 mi^2, and the lower 48 states of the USA have an area of 3.12 million mi^2. Niger would fit into the lower 48 states approximately 6.38 times. Or, the lower 48 states combined are almost 6.4 times larger than the country of Niger.** (Students may wish to calculate the comparison using the entire area of the 50 US states.)

3) How many times would the lower 48 states of the United States fit into the continent of Africa?
The continent of Africa has a land area of 11.7 million mi^2, and the lower 48 states of the USA have an area of 3.12 million mi^2. Dividing 11.7 million mi^2 by 3.12 million mi^2, we find that the lower 48 states would fit into the continent of Africa about 3.75 times. Or, West Africa is nearly 4 times as large as the 48 contiguous states.

4) How many times would West Africa's smallest country, Gambia, fit into your country?
Possible answer for the lower 48 US states: **Gambia has a surface area of 4,360 mi^2, and the lower 48 states of the USA have an area of 3.12 million mi^2. Dividing 3.12 million mi^2 by 4,360 mi^2, we find that Gambia would fit into the USA's lower 48 over 715 times.**

5) Find out the size of your home state. How many times would it fit into the continent of Africa?
Answer for California: **California has a land area of approximately 156,000 mi^2, and the continent of Africa has a land area of 11.7 million mi^2. Dividing 11.7 million mi^2 by 156,000 mi^2, we find that**

the state of California would fit into the continent of Africa about 75 times.

....

SENEGAL

Journal Entry #2
Dakar: Life in the Capital City

1) Who stamps the travelers' passports?
Officers at the airport stamp the traveler's passports.

2) What kind of food did Mabiba plan to cook?
She planned to make Chicken Yassa, a Senegalese sauce made from lemons, dijon mustard, and onions

3) What kinds of things can you find at Dakar's Sandaga Market?
All kinds of things like beads, bananas, sweet potatoes, melons, and onions.

4) What kind of drums do the travelers see at the market?
The travelers see sabar drums.

5) What rhythm did the drummers play?
The drummers played the N'Daaga rhythm

....

Journal Entry #3
Podor: Song of the River

1) What two famous Senegalese musicians come from Podor?
Baaba Maal and Mansour Sek come from Podor.

2) What river runs by Podor?
The Senegal River runs by Podor.

3) What natural rhythms do the travelers observe while they're on the Senegal River?
The travelers observed the bump of the paddle against the wooden side of the boat, the swish of water rushing by, and the rest in between.

4) What is *Kokoriko*?
Kokoriko is the crow of the rooster that wakes people up

5) What is the message of the *Miyaabele* song?
Miyaabele encourages Africans to work together to build a better future.

....

GUINEA

Journal Entry #4
Labé: Blessing from a Djeli

1) How does the village react to the full moon?
The light of the full moon invites everyone to gather outside and make music late into the night.

2) What is the name of the African xylophone?
Bala, or balafon

3) What is a djeli?
A djeli is a traditional musician and history-keeper of West Africa. Many can recite long histories from memory. Djelis inherit their musical status through the family line.

4) What rhythm do the travelers learn?
The travelers learn Lamba.

5) For what purpose do the djelis play Lamba?
Lamba is a rhythm and song performed for djelis. It gives thanks for the gift of music and celebrates the important role of the djeli in keeping the musical traditions of Guinea alive and well.

....

Cultural Connections
The Story of the Balafon

1) What materials are balafons made from?
Balafons are made from numerous slats of hardwood cut into different sizes, tied to a frame made of wood or bamboo. Dried gourds are attached underneath each slat.

2) The balafon is played in which countries?
The balafon is played in Guinea, Burkina Faso, Mali, Côte D'Ivoire, Senegal, Ghana, and Gambia.

3) According to the story recounted above, which kingdom invented the balafon?
The Susu Kingdom invented the balafon.

4) What happened to the original Susu Balafon?
The Mande captured it from the Susu during a war in 1236 A.D. Since around that time, it has been kept in a village in northern Guinea and guarded by a djeli family. The original Susu Bala still exists, and it is brought out and played for very special occasions. It is said that all Mande balafons made today are tuned according to the Susu Bala.

5) Approximately how old is the original Susu Balafon today?
The original Susu Balafon is approximately 800 years old.

....

Journal Entry #5
Kissidougou: Encounter with a Djembefola

1) What instruments are part of the drum ensemble?
Djembes, dundun drums (dundunba, sangban, kenkeni), and bell are part of the drum ensemble.

2) What is a djembefola?
A djembefola is an expert in the art of playing djembe.

3) How many rhythms does the djembefola know?
The djembefola knows more than 100 different rhythms and their uses.

4) Name five different occasions in Guinea where rhythms are played on drums.
In Guinea, rhythms are played for weddings, holidays, festivals, funerals, initiations, planting, the harvest, and all kinds of events in the community

MALI

Journal Entry #6
Bamako: A Wedding in the Capitol City

1) What does the name Bamako mean?
It means "Crocodile River" in the Bambara language.

2) Where is the wedding party set up?
The wedding party is set up under a tent in the middle of the street.

3) Who entertains the wedding party?
Djeli singers and drummers entertain the wedding party.

4) What is the job of the djelis?
The djelis entertain the wedding party by singing songs praising the families joined in marriage. They sing the family history.

5) What types of drums are played at the wedding party?
Djembes, dunduns, and konkoni drums are played at the wedding party.

Journal Entry #7
Sikasso: The Wassoulou Sound of the South

1) What instruments make up the Wassoulou band?
Djembes, dunduns, kariyan scraper, electric guitar, and kamele n'goni make up the Wassoulou band.

2) What topics are commonly discussed in Wassoulou music?
Women's rights, modern families, and marriage are commonly discussed topics in Wassoulou music.

3) How are Wassoulou performers different from djelis?
Djelis must be born into musical families, but Wassoulou performers are musicians by choice, not by birth.

4) Why does Wassoulou music appeal to the younger generation?
Wassoulou music discusses modern themes and it has a good rhythm that makes the music sound good.

Journal Entry #8
Bandiagara Plateau: The Mysterious Dogon

1) Why did the Dogon people first come to the Bandiagara Plateau?
They wanted to escape invaders that threatened their way of life in western Mali. They felt safe in the Bandiagara Plateau area because they could build their houses high up in the cliffs.

2) What do the Dogon houses look like?
Dogon houses are built into the cliffs. They are made of reddish clay, and each one is a little different. They look hand-sculpted by an artist, and some of them have decorations shaped

into the clay, some of them painted red, black, yellow, and white. Each house has its own granary topped with a grass roof that looks like a pointy hat. The nicest buildings have wooden doors carved with scenes of people, animals, and plants.

3) What kind of masks do the travelers see?
They see masks of animals - monkeys, antelopes, snakes, and birds - and Kanaga masks.

4) How do the masks tell their story?
Each of the masks moves around the ceremony area in a way that tells its story through dance.

5) What is the purpose of the mask dance that the travelers witness?
It's purpose is to honor the life of a village elder who recently passed away, and to bring to life the ancestors, animals, plants, and people of the Dogon.

....

NIGER

Journal Entry #9
The Route to Agadez: A Camel Caravan

1) What old caravan route do the travelers cross?
The travelers follow an old caravan route from Gao, Mali, to Agadez, Niger.

2) What were some of the important items of trade for camel caravans?
Some of the important items of trade were gold and salt.

3) What adaptations do camels have for living in the desert?
They have tall, skinny legs to keep them away from the heat of the sand, long eyelashes to keep sun and sand out of their eyes, and a camel hump that stores extra fat and water for long desert crossings.

4) What do the adventurers eat when they are invited to have dinner with the Tuaregs?
They eat a porridge of millet with sweet dates and goat cheese, and finish the meal with three rounds of sweet tea.

5) What instruments do the Tuaregs play after dinner?
They play a calabash drum called a gasu and a mollo, which is like a guitar with three strings.

....

Journal Entry #10
Zinder: The Call of the Kalangou

1) How are the travelers greeted by their friend Adamou?
Adamou greets the travelers in the Hausa language. He says, "Sannu da zuwa!" which means "Welcome!" Then they exchange traditional greetings like "How is your family?" and "How is your work?"

2) What is the response to the Hausa greetings?
The response is always "Lafiya lo!" or, "In health!"

3) How does the kalangou imitate speech?
The drummer can change the pitch of the drum by squeezing its sides while playing, creating a "talking" effect.

4) How are the guards of the Sultan dressed?

The guards of the Sultan wear long robes in bright colors of red, yellow, and green, topped with red turbans.

5) What is the function of the Sultan?
The Sultan acts as a regional king, and he can make legal decisions that affect the people of his kingdom.

....

Journal Entry #11
Larba Birno: The Rhythms of Village Life

1) What are some of the sounds that the travelers hear in the morning?
The travelers hear the sound of a rooster crowing, the wooden pounding of a mortar and pestle as a woman grinds grain for the morning meal, the squeaking wheels of a donkey cart passing by, the hooves of a donkey clomping along in rhythm, buckets of water sloshing from a well, and birds twittering from a tree.

2) How do people greet each other in West Africa?
It's considered polite in West Africa to take your time and properly greet people by asking about their family, their health, their business, and life in general before moving on to any other discussion.

3) How many rounds of tea do the travelers drink with Udu?
They drink three rounds of tea.

4) What happens when the drummers start to play?
The drummers play a dance rhythm, and the beat calls people from their homes. They form a circle of dancers around the drummers and take turns in the middle of the circle, showing off their dance moves.

....

BURKINA FASO

Journal Entry #12
Ouagadougou: The Language of Dance

1) Describe the taxi that the travelers take from Niger to Burkina Faso.
The travelers take a bush taxi from Niger to Burkina Faso. It's a 12-seat passenger van overloaded with 24 people and a couple of chickens, stacked with baggage, onions, chickens, and live sheep tied to the top.

2) How does the name Burkina Faso translate to English?
Burkina Faso translates to "Country of the People with Integrity".

3) What is FESPACO?
FESPACO is Africa's largest and most important film festival, attended by filmmakers and movie buffs from all over Africa and the world. It is an international festival that happens in Ouagadougou every two years.

4) Which percussion instruments are part of Aisha's performance group?
balafons, djembes, dunduns, and a gita

5) What do the dancers express in their performance?
The dancers tell a story of what life is like in a traditional village in Burkina Faso. Through dance, they express activities including planting seeds, harvesting crops, pounding grain,

making a fire, cooking, carrying water, caring for children, celebrating, competing, and a masquerade dance.

....

Journal Entry #13
Boni: Masters of the Masquerade

1) What kinds of things are being sold at the market in Boni?
Merchants are selling things like fruit, rice, spices, fabric, and cooking pots.

2) About how tall is the serpent mask?
The travelers think the serpent mask is at least 15 feet tall.

3) What types of animal masks do the travelers see?
They see masks of antelopes, hyenas, buffaloes, monkeys, bush pigs, crocodiles, fish, hawks, and butterflies.

4) How do the different masks dance?
Each of the masks dances in a way that mimics the behavior of the animal. The antelope bucks, prances, and stamps his feet, making a great show of his beautiful horns. The butterfly, covered in an impressive pattern of eight targets, twirls left and right, then comes to rest as if perched on a flower before flying away again. The bush pig paws at the ground with his feet, throwing up clouds of dust, and sniffing the air for the scent of danger.

5) What musical instruments accompany the mask dance in Boni?
The masquerade is accompanied by an ensemble of musicians playing high-pitched whistles, balafons, and two types of drums: a long, skinny drum like a big kalangou and a round bass drum like the doumdoum from Niger.

....

Journal Entry #14
Bobo-Dioulasso: Burkina's Musical Heartland

1) What do the travelers say is remarkable about Bobo-Dioulasso?
Bobo-Dioulasso is remarkable for its rich tradition of drum and dance ensembles.

2) How have the performing groups evolved to a very high level of accomplishment in Bobo?
Performance groups sprout up all over the city and compete with each other to be the best. This competitive tradition has a long history in Bobo, and as a result, the drum and dance groups have developed a very high level of skill and talent.

3) What are many of the groups aiming to accomplish?
Every time a group performs, they are aiming to be the best. They hope for an opportunity to make it big with a world tour, a record deal, or another breakthrough like that.

4) What instruments are played by the performing group?
The group plays djembes, dunduns, and balafon.

5) What shows the ensemble that they have been successful tonight?
The participation of the audience is proof that they have succeeded tonight, even without a major breakthrough.

ABOUT THE AUTHORS

Dancing Drum's mission is to *educate, entertain,* and *inspire* people of all ages through interactive, percussion-based programs. Much of the content presented in Dancing Drum's programs and publications has been gathered during research travels in Africa, the Caribbean, Asia, and throughout the US.

With over 25 years of drumming experience between them, Steve Campbell and Lindsay Rust (co-founders of Dancing Drum) have immersed themselves in many styles of world percussion. The music of West Africa has always been a source of great inspiration for both, and they have made several trips to the region to study the music and cultural arts directly at the source.

Steve and Lindsay's West African travel adventures are the inspiration for "The Rhythm Hunters" - the narrative thread that runs through this book's Journal Entries, tying the music, art, and cultural content together. Through the Rhythm Hunters, months of travels have been condensed into 14 action-packed stories for students to read and enjoy.

Steve Campbell

Steve is an accomplished musician, well-versed in many percussive arts including drum set, mallet percussion, West African and Caribbean drumming. He holds a Bachelor of Arts degree from the University of California Santa Barbara and a California Multi-Subject Teaching Credential. His skill as a percussionist is matched only by his excellence at teaching and inspiring students of all ages.

Lindsay Rust

Lindsay has been teaching, performing and developing curriculum content with Dancing Drum since the beginning in 2002. Her extensive experience in West Africa includes over 2 years serving in the Peace Corps in Niger, managing an award-winning Afropop band from Niger, a double major in Anthropology and Art Theory & Practice from Northwestern University, and years of study and performance of percussive arts.

SELECTED BIBLIOGRAPHY

Bebey, Francis. African Music: A People's Art. Chicago: Lawrence Hill Books, 1975.

Billmeier, Uschi. Mamady Keita: A Life for the Djembe. Brussels: Arun-Verlag, 1999.

Bovin, Mette. Nomads Who Cultivate Beauty: Woodabe Dances and Visual Arts in Niger. Nordiska Afrikainstitutet, Uppsala, Sweden, 2001.

Burkina Faso: A Welcome Book. Ouagadougou: Peace Corps Burkina Faso, 2006

Burns, James and Collins, Robert. A History of Sub-Saharan Africa. Cambridge: Cambridge University Press, 2007.

Charry, Eric. Mande Music. Chicago: the University of Chicago Press, 2000.

CIA World Factbook Online. July 1, 2010 <www.cia.gov/library/publications/the-world-factbook/index.html>

Conrad, David. Sunjata: A West African Epic of the Mande Peoples. Indianapolis: Hackett Publishing Company, 2004.

Decalo, James. Historical Dictionary of Niger. Scarecrow Press/ Metuchen. NJ - London, 1979.

Dieterlen, Germaine. "Masks and Mythology Among the Dogon" African Arts. vol. 21, no. 4 (1988)

Eyre, Banning. "Mali on the Mall." Afropop Worldwide. July 1, 2010 <www.Afropop.org>

Fuuta Jalon: A Brief History. July 10, 2010 <www.fuuta-jalon.net>

Griaule, Marcel and Dieterlen, Germaine. "The Dogon" African Worlds: Studies in the Cosmological Ideas and Social Values of African Peoples, 1954.

Hahner-Herzog, Iris. African Masks from the Barbier-Mueller Collection. Geneva: Prestel Publishing, 1997.

Jessup, Lynne. The Mandinka Balafon. La Mesa, CA: Xylo Publications, 2008.

Midho Waawi Pular! Learner's Guide to Pular. Conakry: Peace Corps Guinea, 2006.

Owusu, Heike. Symbols of Africa. New York: Sterling Publishing Company, 2000.

Parkenham, Thomas. The Scramble for Africa. New York: Avon Books, 1991.

Pittman, Todd. "West Africa's Giraffes Make a Big Comeback: Niger Uses Carrots (loans, tourism), Sticks (prison, fines) to Help Population" Associated Press: 11/7/2009

Redmond, Lane. When the Drummers Were Women. New York: Three Rivers Press, 1997.

Roy, Christopher. "Adulthood." Art and Life in Africa Online. ed. Lee McIntyre and Christopher Roy. 1998. University of Iowa. July 10, 2010 <http://www.uiowa.edu/~africart/toc/chapters/kml/adulthood.html>

Savage, Andrew. "Writing Tuareg — the three script options" International Journal of the Sociology of Language. 192 (2008): 5-14

Smithsonian Human Origins Program. Smithsonian Institution. June 20, 2010 <www.humanorigins.si.edu/education>

Sublette, Ned. Cuba & Its Music: From the First Drums to the Mambo. Chicago Review Press. Chicago, 2007.

Survival Wolof. Dakar: Peace Corps Senegal, 2006.

Tang, Patricia. Masters of the Sabar: Wolof Griot Percussionists of Senegal. Philadelphia: Temple University Press, 2007.

World Music, the Rough Guide: Africa, Europe and the Middle East. New York: Penguin Books USA, 2000.

RESOURCES FOR TEACHERS

Other Publications by Dancing Drum:

Drumming Up Character: A Hip-Hop Music Approach to Character Education

Drum, dance, and sing your way through 10 positive character traits. Featuring upbeat hip-hop music, character raps, and reading and art activities, teachers can use this book to stage a student show and build a character education program for ages 6-12.

Teacher's Guide
142 pgs, CD & DVD
Item # DD-DUC-TBK
ISBN 978-0-9816724-0-3

Student Workbook, 76 pgs
Item # DD-DUC-SBK
ISBN 978-0-9816724-1-0

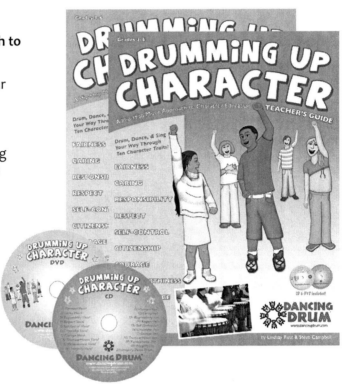

Community Drum Ensemble: Volume 1

Featuring 6 world music arrangements for djembe, djun-djun, and hand percussion, plus full instructions for beginning a Community Drum Ensemble program in your school or community! For ages 12-adult.

72 pgs, CD & DVD
Item # DD-CDE-V1
ISBN 978-0-9816724-2-7

School Drum Packages:

Dancing Drum's djembes, djun-djuns, and drum accessories are designed for the needs of schools. Combining durability, ease of use, and affordability with the finest quality construction, these instruments offer the best combination of quality and value available today. Constructed from sustainably harvested hardwood, our drums are made to last for many years of playing.

Drum packages are available for any size of classroom. Visit our website at www. dancingdrum.com for more information, sound samples, and package options. Schools are eligible to receive a 10% discount on all of the listed prices.

12-student school drum package with 3 djun-djuns (dundunba, sangban, kenkeni), 3 djembes (13", 11", 9"), 3 pairs of claves, 3 pairs of maracas, an agogo bell, drum stands, drum bags, & sticks

Programs for Schools:

SCHOOL ASSEMBLIES | ARTIST-IN-RESIDENCY | WORKSHOP-TO-PERFORMANCE TEACHER TRAINING | DRUM CIRCLES & WORKSHOPS

Dancing Drum travels about 6 months out of the year to bring our programs to schools across the country. Sign up for our mailing list to find out when we'll be coming to your area by sending an email to info@dancingdrum.com.

For more information, contact: info@dancingdrum.com, call (805) 682.8250, or mail Dancing Drum | P.O. Box 91841 | Santa Barbara, CA | 93190-1841

CD Tracks

1-11 SENEGAL	12-22 GUINEA	23-33 MALI	34-44 NIGER	45-55 BURKINA FASO
N'Daaga Drum	*Lamba Drum*	*Didadi Drum*	*Takamba Drum*	*Makossa Drum*
1) Level 1	12) Level 1	23) Level 1	34) Level 1	45) Level 1
2) Level 2	13) Level 2	24) Level 2	35) Level 2	46) Level 2
3) Level 3	14) Level 3	25) Level 3	36) Level 3	47) Level 3
4) Drum Break	15) Drum Break	26) Drum Break	37) Drum Break	48) Drum Break
5) Level 4	16) Level 4	27) Level 4	38) Level 4	49) Level 4
Miyaabele Xylo	*Lamba Xylo*	*Didadi Xylo*	*Takamba Xylo*	*Makossa Xylo*
6) Level 1	17) Level 1	28) Level 1	39) Level 1	50) Level 1
7) Level 2	18) Level 2	29) Level 2	40) Level 2	51) Level 2
8) Level 3	19) Level 3	30) Level 3	41) Level 3	52) Level 3
9) Level 4	20) Level 4	31) Level 4	42) Level 4	53) Level 4
10) Level 5	21) Level 5	32) Level 5	43) Level 5	54) Level 5
11) Break Ending	22) Break Ending	33) Break Ending	44) Break Ending	55) Break Ending

DVD Tracks

THE MUSIC	DVD CONNECTIONS	VISUAL ART PROJECTS	PRONUNCIATION GUIDE
Senegal	Bamako Wedding	*Senegal*	Countries
N'Daaga Drum	Didadi Dance	Paper Bead Mask	Music Titles
Miyaabele Xylo	Cross of Agadez	*Guinea*	Instruments
Guinea	Tifinagh Alphabet	Djembefola Hat	
Lamba Drum	*Gasu* Calabash Drum	*Mali*	**DRUM FUNDAMENTALS**
Lamba Xylo	*Kalangou* Talking Drum	Dogon Kanaga Mask	Djembe
Mali	A Day in the Village	*Niger*	Djun-Djun
Didadi Drum	The Language of Dance	Woodabe Pouch	Teaching Tools
Didadi Xylo	Bwa Masquerade	*Burkina Faso*	
Niger	Les Bambous	Bwa Hawk Mask	
Takamba Drum			
Takamba Xylo			
Burkina Faso			
Makossa Drum			
Makossa Xylo			

NOTE: "Drumming Up World Music: West Africa" should include a **CD and DVD**. If there are no discs attached inside the cover of this book, email **info@dancingdrum. com** to request your copies at no additional charge. Please include your shipping address, and let us know where you purchased the book.